I0525431

Lilika and Other Journeys

Stories and Poetry

HD Russell

Copyright © 2014 by Heather Russell
All rights reserved.
ISBN: 0991618009
ISBN-13: 978-0-9916180-0-2

This is a work of fiction. Any and all names, characters, places, and situations, other than those which are public domain are a product of the author's imagination and are not intended to resemble actual persons, living or dead. Locations and events are entirely coincidental.

AKNOWLEDGEMENTS

The undertaking of this book was massive and took place of over the course of several years. A lot of people have gotten me to this point all of whom I owe a huge debt of gratitude. I should start with my loving and supportive wife. She is my support and critic in just the right balance. She has never stopped encouraging me to pursue my dreams. Anytime and every time she is there to tell me that I am indeed doing the right thing in trying to be not only a writer but an author. Sarah is my one true love and I would be nowhere and nothing without her. For years I said I would change everything about my life but now I wouldn't change a thing because I may not have her if I did.

The second person I have to give major gratitude is Travis Sherfey. Not only has he been my best friend since high school but he helped format this book to give it a proper shape and form. He made me clarify what was obviously only clear in my head. He has been my biggest emotional backer and lucky for those around us can see through my bullshit. He is not just a friend but a soul brother if ever there was such a thing.

I would be remiss if I went without acknowledging friends and family who have watched me struggle with this life and never let me forget that I do indeed have an outlet and a talent. They are there to laugh with and at me. To drink when we need a drink and eat good food when we need good food. Everyone I know has helped make this possible in some fashion and I am so very grateful. Thank you all.

Contents

Section I
The Journey of Lilika
The Chase of a Soul

Prologue

"The sunshine is lovely today," Jordana said looking at the sky then to the woman by her side. For her part Adriana stared at the water. "This is a lovely park. Very conducive to our conversation." Adriana's voice smiled as she said the word conversation.

They shifted on the bench, their knees touching then separating. Adriana sighed. After all this time the sexual tension remained steadily flowing behind every word, every accidental brush of skin, or every time blue eyes met brown.

Jordana breathed a deep ragged breath. "Our time in this life has passed. We shouldn't push it anymore."

"That's it then?" Adriana stood up.

"You have too many questions and you refuse all the answers. Your instability and naïveté show more than you think." Jordana smiled and looked up at Adriana. The sound of laughter from behind them caused Jordana to stand and turn quickly around. "Uncle Ares," Jordana spat, "still wearing leather I see."

"Still wearing human flesh?" Ares verbally shot back.

Adriana stood motionless then whispered, "Who? What?"

Ares walked around the bench and come to stand in front of them. "Well at least she isn't ugly like the last time."

Jordana rolled her eyes. "Get to the point. Quickly."

"Give *her* a message for me," Ares said emphasizing her. "Tell her I have three and when it's five the world is mine." He then disappeared in a flash of blue and silver light.

Jordana turned completely around ignoring Adriana's stuttered syllables and shock. Jordana put her hand to her temples feeling the blood pulsating. This had officially ruined what was already going to be a heart wrenching occasion. "Adriana, I have to make a phone call then we have a great deal more to talk about." Adriana shook her head and followed Jordana to the parking lot. Jordana looked up to the sky, smelling the air before climbing into the driver's side of the car. "Rains' coming."

Jordana dialed the phone once seated in the car. In the back of her mind she expected the worst. If her uncle was sending a message to Lexia, the mysterious *her*, after not disobeying Zeus on this for more than 1,000 years then what ever he was planning must be more than deadly. Unlike his previous bumblings and practical jokes in the past, he seemed to have a new determination. Now, Adriana was involved and could be used as leverage.

"Yes, I need to place a trans-Atlantic call."

Adriana sat listening and not believing any of it but knowing it to be the truth. She nearly exited the car and only stopped when Jordana's hand caught her by the arm. Jordana smiled looking directly into her eyes Adriana dropped her chin and returned the smile.

Jordana continued the conversation, apparently connected with the mysterious her. "Gelly, hey...yes it really has been..." Jordana smiled.

"Oh I wish I were calling for a little wine and dancing..." she said with a short laugh and brief pause. "Well, the dances are dreary compared to the last time we met, yet oddly familiar..." Adriana listened to the laugh and wondered at the secret. Mysterious wasn't a word she would have used for Jordana before today. She thought they knew each other completely, even if they only saw each other occasionally. Though they lived separate lives they loved one another wholly. She continued listening to the half of the conversation she could hear.

"I was paid a visit today by Ares...yes...where is she?" Jordana listened then interrupted the person on the other end. "Yes, I'm going to call some help...Look he said he has three and when he has five..." She trailed off and shook her head, the person on the other end having finished the sentence. "Get her the message and be at my house in two days. If it is what you said then we may not have as much to fear. I have a piece...All right. Two days. Until then." She disconnected the line.

Adriana sighed as Jordana cut the phone off. She couldn't hide her confusion.

"I suppose you would like and explanation?" Adriana shook her head yes. She didn't trust her voice not to betray the fear that was tickling the back of her brain. If Ares managed to rebuild this machine there would be no end to the evil he could put upon the world. Jordana shook her head and said, "I need to get some stuff in order and I will tell you a story, my story, which you may come to know as your own. I will bring us to these moments and see if it goes beyond."

Chapter 1 The Beginning

"I suppose an introduction would be the best way to begin. My proper name is Lilika. Those who know me well call me by this name. This story will contain incidents and people you may not or are not willing to believe happened or exist. Let me and what you witnessed be what you put your trust in. Eventually everyone must tell their life story to a stranger or a friend, maybe both in this case. I can't pretend not to be excited." Lilika smiled at this. "What you witnessed—possibly what brought us to this very moment—is my aunties, The Fates. At least they had a hand in it, I'm sure. I am a Greek Goddess." Upon a skeptical look from Adriana she said, "So you haven't heard of me? That doesn't make me a liar. History hasn't heard of a thousand gods. Time has lost a million gods—that doesn't mean we do not exist.

"My birth was as ridiculous as my conception but it is mine. I was born to Aphrodite. I'm the youngest of all gods who isn't a demi-god, the beautiful accident after a godly celebration with too much wine and ambrosia. The other party involved was Artemis. A drunken argument, some accidental words, and a short time later there I was. Aphrodite, Mom, raised me. My brother,

Eros, was nearly grown so we were wonderfully close. Artemis, Mother, wasn't absent, just busy. She was always there if called and loved me as she loved the spring time. She made me strong and capable while mom showed me how to relax. My grandfather, Zeus, took special interest in me. He showed me our kingdom. 'This is our time,' he would say with such conviction. It wasn't until millennia later I understood the sadness in his eyes. The fall of the Greek gods was an easy one. Not fatal, and only dramatic because they made it so. I say *they* because I was occupied and remained uninvolved though I did get an earful later.

"My story, on the other hand, is dramatic and beautiful and contains human masks that span more than two thousand years. I just hope my words suffice. Who knows, maybe you'll learn something from the goddess with the gorgeous bod, rock star hair, and beautiful black and teal wings." Lilika winked at the girl who had a less than open look on her beautiful features.

"Yes, well, I'll get on with the story. I was born and subsequently grew up. Mt. Olympus was my home for that time. After growing up, it was let slip by a drunken chronicling priestess of Mom's that I existed. In those days there was a god for almost everything— real or not. This was a long time before Solon and his democracy. I'll keep you guessing about how long only because history is still incomplete. Anyway, a small sect of beautiful people became my followers. Bless'd Be the homosexuals I always say. I wasn't flashy like Mom but I was fair in answering prayers. It was wonderful fun. My life was unattached and beautiful. As a god I wasn't for nothing, answering prayers, attending parties given by mortals and immortals alike. Observing humanity, being privy to the secrets humanity kidded themselves over. I thought my life was blissfully complete.

"Then at a mortal gala thrown by a very rich man blessed by us many times over I met a girl. The youngest child of this man who was herself called Adelphie. He lavished affection upon her. I didn't exactly meet her at the gala so much as outside of it. Adelphie was his only daughter and was set to be his caretaker when he became old and invalid. She was the youngest and so not sacrificed at birth but instead rejoiced in. She was as educated as any man and beautiful. He refused to force her into a marriage so she felt no need to be in society. Adelphie was sixteen when we met. I spied her laying on a fountain wall in a private courtyard. Her eyes were closed and she was humming with the music that could be heard from inside. I shook my wings and took a drink of water.

"Goddess!" She jumped to her feet startled then bowed her head. When our eyes met I became paralyzed. When I came to my senses I shook my head clear and smiled.

"Don't be startled. Please sit." I gestured to the wall with my hand. I folded my wings and sat opposite her. When she looked up at me I realized she was waiting for me to speak so she didn't speak out of turn. Thus began the conversation that would carry me across two millennia.

"You are the daughter he speaks so kindly of? The one who refuses society?" I laughed.

"Adelphie became hesitant then shook her head. I pressed on even though I would never have before. Unless it was for business, and I knew immediately this was for pleasure. I can be kind, but never could be accused of benevolence for no reason. I decided to jump in and ask the tough questions. She was young. She could handle it. "Do you not want the life you are presented with?" I tried to keep my tone light. I didn't want to scare her. She spoke quickly, saying, "No, that isn't it. My father will need me. His eyes are already weak."

"I smiled. "It was a little much though, wasn't it?" I said referring to the party inside. She laughed and I knew I couldn't be all that scary.

"Yes, almost no redeeming factors." As she

laughed and spoke I saw a little of what grandfather saw in mortals. Their beauty. The ultimate fatality is the death of that beauty. The growing old and withering of it. That is how it is meant to be. Mortals were made to be disposable, with the soul reusable. In that moment I understood why they hold on so tightly and make so many nonsense rules among themselves even though they have no real power.

"So what will you do with all your time if not filling it was a husband and children?"

"She looked as though she had never really thought about it. "I will continue to learn. I will feed the poor and help people."

"I don't know if I smiled at this or if I wasn't as flippant as I remember. "All very noble," I said. "A noble waste of time."

"She looked away in shock that her answer did not impress me. "There will always be poor people. It will always get worse. Even if you use up all of your father's assets, what will that do but make you poor?"

"She fired back immediately forgetting her shyness, "We must do what we can! We lowly mortals do not have the luxury of doing nothing. We must fight for our survival!"

"I came back at her enjoying this side of her. "No, you don't. I witness every day mortals who ignore what is wrong and do nothing with their time but enjoy it to the fullest of their capabilities. Young. Old. Rich, and yes, the poor." She sat back down having jumped to her feet during her rant. I smiled. "You were made to make the best of it. Those who realize that are always better off."

"Just then a servant girl came outside to say that Adelphie's evening meal was prepared and in her rooms.

"Good bye, Adelphie. We must argue again sometime." I stretched my wings and flew into the sky. Adelphie sighed with frustration as she walked inside. I decided right then that was the most I had ever enjoyed myself. She stood up to me, a lovely surprise. As I made rounds at the temple that night I couldn't stop thinking of the spunky little mortal. She had absolutely caught my attention and wasn't letting go.

"A week passed and I was at the temple looking over offerings, eating fruit and all the usual things, when I heard a familiar voice from behind.

"Lilika. Daughter."

"I turned around and said, "Yo, Mom." She walked over to the table.

"Anything good?"

"No, same old same old," I said absentmindedly.

"You left in a hurry from the party the other day,"

she said making a point to look me in the face.

"There wasn't anything to hold my attention," I said inspecting a particularly gaudy piece of jewelry. I was trying to figure out if it was a necklace, a head dress, or maybe even a baby belt. I sat it down. 'Should I have stayed?' I turned to face her. She smiled. The way she smiles when she has a secret. I raised my eyebrows. I knew she would spill it.

"If you would have read what that girl wrote," she squealed with laughter. "Later!" I hadn't counted on her being cryptic. I'll admit to some intrigue at that point. So I did the god thing and showed up without her knowing I was in the room.

"She was having her noon meal alone, once again. Her father has spent the day out or in meetings. Aside from servants, she was alone. I sat on the couch opposite her using this time to study her. Adelphie's eyes were a deep chocolate in contrast to her flaxen hair. As I watched her eat I noticed her harp-shaped mouth was delicate; her lower lip lined up perfectly with her chin. Her fingers were long but not slight, plump enough to still only be sixteen. Her nose was straight and narrow which suited her almond shaped eyes. When she finished her meal she stretched and yawned. I almost left, assuming she would nap. Instead she went to her desk to retrieve her writings. I walked over and stood just behind her right shoulder. She began to write but not about me. I read every word, standing behind her well into the evening. When the servants brought her food and lit the lamps, she rose and stretched then put her writings away.

"They were merely observations of the idle rich, a lot of misconception and humanity. They meant something to her, though, and so would come to mean a great deal to me. I came back several more times over the course of the next year never revealing my presence. Occasionally, she would wonder about me in her writings but I never would involve myself in her affairs.

"As her brothers had children, three having children in the same season, I saw her grow close to the children and her brother's wives. While she had always been close with her father, Adelphie and her brothers never bonded. The closer she became to her brother's wives and children, the more she began to reflect on her own life. In that time, at seventeen by now, she knew those were dreams of a life she shouldn't hope for. She couldn't imagine someone ruling over her and being an ordinary house wife.

"A year to the day that she laid eyes on me, I found myself watching her from her balcony. I stayed in the shadows careful not to let her notice me. The sun was setting and the servants were moving about the rooms lighting lamps. As I watched the servants from the corner of my eye, I saw a flash of metal. Adelphie said loudly, "Who are you and how did you come to be on my balcony?"

I stepped from the shadows and she put the dagger down.

"I do apologize, Goddess." I laughed. She smiled. "I knew I would see you today." She didn't bow her head this time but she couldn't meet my eyes, either.

"I told you I wanted to argue again sometime." I sat on a pillowed couch and motioned for her to sit as well. She laughed and that pleased me more than I can explain.

"So you wish to argue with me?" The servants brought her wine as she tried unsuccessfully to relax.

"What will we argue about?" I asked, taking a sip of the wine. I took another sip; it was cold and deliciously chilled by the river. "The weather?"

"She sat her glass down. "You want to argue about the weather?"

"I laughed, realizing it sounded ridiculous. "All right," I said. "Is there not something you've always wanted to ask the gods, or in this case the beautiful goddess before you?" I gestured to her desk. Her eyes grew wide and I braced for an argument. Instead she sighed loudly and smiled. Slowly her excitement bubbled up as she realized the opportunity.

"While she thought, it came to me suddenly that she may never lose the wonder and the fear of me. I didn't like this thought and tried to put it out of my mind. I didn't want that pious fire to burn in her. I didn't want her piousness in any form. I wanted her love and friendship. Not worship. While she thought and thought, I thought and debated. I debated my pursuit of her over the last year. I debated giving up. When she looked at me I knew I would not.

"Finally she spoke. "How did all of this come to be?"

I frowned. "That is a common question. One for which you know the answer. It is unimportant. Ask me how it ends."

"She inhaled shaking her head. "All right. So how it began is of no consequence? Yet how it ends is?"

"I stayed coy. I wanted this to last. I wanted her to be unimpressed with me. "Well the beginning matters, just not yet."

"When?"

"Roughly?" I asked causing her impatience to

grow as my amusement grew. "Fine, four thousand years or so."

"She looked as though I had slapped her. "Why so long from now?" As she asked I realized she couldn't really conceive it.

"You wouldn't believe me. Does it matter?" She appeared offended by my words. She then jumped to her feet looking at me in an accusatory manner. "But you are a goddess! You wouldn't lie to a..." She stopped, turning crimson, but I heard what she meant to say.

"To a what?" I wanted to hear her say it.

"A human," she shouted.

"Say what you mean, Adelphie. You were going to say follower. I know about your visits to my temple."

"She interrupted me. "I know you've watched me. Even when I couldn't see you I felt you!" She quieted to a whisper. "Why?" I looked up at her, at the tears in her eyes. I stood putting my face directly in front of hers so close we breathed the same air.

I told her quietly, "Your view of the gods is askew. We do lie." She searched my eyes then saw the truth. "I've harmed you." It was a statement, an admission on my part. To show her I had a heart, a heart to love her.

"No, I've harmed myself." She answered my

admission with one of her own. I left the way I came without another word.

"Immediately I went to find Aphrodite. It didn't take long. She was standing on the steps looking at all the virgins sitting there.

"Hey, daughter, why so glum?" She was inspecting the girls even though they had no idea.

"I just saw Adelphie," I said taking a seat on the steps above the girls.

"This is your own fault, kid," she said. I sighed. Even if she had a point I didn't see it at the time. I knew something bigger was happening.

"I can't help my own feelings, Mom. Besides, it worked out for Eros."

"She couldn't argue with that but she tried. "You aren't your brother, Lil, and you are more like your Mother than you should be. If you want her, be with her. Otherwise, stop meddling and leave her alone." I looked at her for a long time. She spoke the truth which was rare when she gave advice on the heart. I think she knew it would be a good show no matter the outcome.

"I spent the night pacing. I drew pros and cons on the wall of my temple. By the morning I still hadn't made a decision. I was in the middle of making another list when I heard a knock at the door. It was the head priestess. She came to tell me there was a girl demanding to see me.

"Tell her I'm not here." I was in no mood to be disturbed.

"She says she feels your presence, Goddess."

"I turned from the priestess and waved for Adelphie to be let in. Before the priestess could leave the room I disappeared. I couldn't see her. I had never had to follow my heart. I never had to make a decision other than to answer which prayer. In the year that followed, I abandoned the temples. I answered prayers from afar. Adelphie became a fervent follower. Her beauty seemed to grow daily, and after a few months she stopped asking about me. She knew that I was watching. Time seemed to go quickly. Then one day, as the year had almost passed, Adelphie didn't come to the temple. The next day passed without her appearance. On the anniversary of the last time we had spoken I found myself once more on her balcony.

"At first I didn't see her, but as I walked on in to her rooms I realized they had been destroyed. Everything was strewn about the room. She had broken her water pots. Ink stained the wall where she had thrown the wells. All of her writings were torn or cast off on the floors. I walked into the room where she slept. She was sprawled across the bed in a drunken sleep. Wine bottles were on the bed and floor, all empty. I called for a servant to tell me what happened, though I knew.

"She's been this way for three days now. She's not eating, only drinking the wine. Then this morning when she realized the day, she flew into a rage destroying everything." The servant kept her head bowed as she spoke.

"Does her father know?"

"No, he has been away this last month."

I dismissed the servant and looked around the room. I had wronged her by staying away. I said it out loud but she was still drunk, still asleep. Selfish worry had let me see her but not let her see me. I waved my hand to clean the room then took a seat on the bed. She moaned in her sleep but showed no signs of waking. Since I had cleaned the rooms, I got a cloth and put it in cold water for her head. She groaned and moved her face from the light of the lamps. I began to study her face. The curve of her cheek and nose. How the corners of her mouth turned up slightly even if she wasn't smiling.

"I stared until the lamp burned itself out. I stared until the lamp burned itself out twice more. I sat at the foot of the bed determined to face her to apologize, to make right the last year of wrong. So lost in thought I was that I didn't hear her wake nor did I see her sit up.

"You disappeared." The hurt was evident though she tried to hide it.

"I did." I was handing her a glass of water when the extraordinary took place. Our fingers met on the glass and nothing short of electricity passed between us and the truth was shown. It was cliché; possibly the origin of cliché. As our eyes met the words *soul mate* passed silently between us. In that instant I was made a helpless god brought to my knees by the very Fates I was kin to.

The irony doesn't escape me; even now it haunts me. I withdrew my hand after glimpsing eternity and sat back on the couch. The universe had collapsed and expanded in an instant. Adelphie smiled. "I love you.'"

Chapter 2 Thickness

"How does that bring us to now?" Adriana asked.

Lilika laughed at the impatient American girl. "Well, it doesn't. That isn't the end. It's very truly the beginning."

"But you're serious? This is a real story? You are who you say you are? That man was your uncle and a god?" Adriana only saw the humanity that was ever-present in Jordana's eyes, not the goddess that lurked behind them. As far as Adriana was concerned, she had her god. He was invisible and lived in a church or in a very exclusive heaven. If you talked to him it was ok, but if he spoke to you then people called you crazy. It was all very confusing and useless as far as Lilika was concerned.

"It's fine that you don't believe me. I can prove it." Lilika stood and in the blink of an eye began a transformation. Where there had been a button down shirt and jeans became sandals and a deep red tunic with a shiny silver breast plate. Pale skin became tanned with a sun-kissed sheen. Lilika's hair went from chin length to a spiked faux hawk the color of dark soil with golden strands interwoven. Black wings appeared behind her shoulders protruding from where shoulder blades had been. When she stretched them the span was longer than the goddess was tall and black everywhere but the wings that lined the bottom which were a deep beautiful teal.

Adriana covered her face with her hands. Lilika sat down beside her. "It doesn't change anything. It only reveals more of the truth." She didn't touch Adriana for fear the girl would pull away. The pair sat in silence. Lilika wanted to continue but chose to wait for Adriana to figure out where to start with the inevitable questions. Lilika made the decision then that, along with words and the godly reveal, she would show Adriana the truth and give her the choice to stay. She was after all in danger now so why not give her a choice? "I want you to come with me to my house. To Greece."

Adriana broke her reverie and looked at Lilika.

"We are at your house." Her voice was hollow and didn't betray the storm that was raging behind her eyes.

"This is Jordana's house. My mortal counterpart, if you will. My house is on a high, beautiful cliff by the sea." Lilika smiled.

"What happens to this house? To your...her...family? Do they know who you really are?"

Lilika had hoped Adriana wouldn't have the courage to ask even though she should have known better. She wanted to reveal these answers in the story.

"They do not know who or what I am. I will form a new Jordana and leave her with the kiss of my essence as a substitute for the soul she lost in losing me. She will have no knowledge of either of us. Should you choose to stay which could be dangerous and not go with me, you will have no knowledge of her." Adriana nodded. Lilika raised her eyebrow and gave a small smile of nothing personal. Adriana had guessed at the answer Lilika supposed, after all it wasn't the first time she has heard this. It had happened more than once in their history together. Lilika should have known her inquisitive nature wouldn't change despite the soul's fleshy outerwear.

Lilika motioned for Adriana to stand. Slowly, the figure of a woman began to appear on the couch. Hazy and transparent, then the details started to emerge. The curve of the cheek and the color of the hair, the roundness of two small but full breasts and the faint pink of the nipples starting to rise and fall as if in a deep sleep. Lilika waved her hand and the clothes she had been wearing not an hour earlier appeared on the sleeping form. Lilika nodded in approval and turned to Adriana. "What do you think?"

Adriana stared at the sleeping Jordana. "Marvelous," she whispered.

Lilika smiled and bent over the newly formed figure, kissing her firmly on the mouth and thereby transferring the smallest of her essence and ensuring Jordana didn't wake up a soulless thing without conscience.

"It is finished. We must go."

***

They exited the house and Lilika turned to Adriana. "I need you to close your eyes. You have chosen to go, yes?"

Adriana nodded the affirmative only hesitating for a moment.

"There are a few ways to do this but we are taking the most direct route since time is of the essence. This may tingle a bit."

The world flashed green and they were gone from the spot. When they appeared a moment later, Adriana opened her eyes and they were in front of a massive ornately designed gate. There were stone walls that were, by her estimate, ten feet high until they turned the corner and became at least fifteen feet high. The walls were painted with ancient figures demonstrating different actions. One was a woman pouring water into a large pot over an open fire. Another was dancing around an open flame with several other women who, even for ancient times, seemed to be dressed oddly. Adriana took a deep breath. It was actually in front of her. She reached out and ran her hand over the gate and touched the wall.

"This is my home. Down the path behind us is a village. It is hidden from the world and completely self-sufficient. You'll love it. The people are free to come and go as they please, but unless one knows where to look it can't be found." Lilika pushed open the gate and held her hand out for Adriana to enter.

"This is the garden. Up this stone path is the courtyard and the doors to all the rooms." Lilika smiled. They made their way up the path, which had a small upward slant, to the open entrance of the courtyard. Adriana started at the size of the courtyard and house surrounding it. In the center lay a huge rectangular fountain with a statue of a beautifully painted woman wearing a tunic of deep purple dressed in the style as the figures painted on the outside walls. Adriana stared at the woman's face; she thought she knew her, so familiar she looked. The woman's jawline, her eyes and the curls falling into them, and the way her lips upturned in a slight smile even when she wasn't smiling. She shook her head. *It must be*

Adelphie, she thought. Around the fountain was grass that met with cement where the entranceways to the doors began, and the second story walkway acted as a first floor overhang. There were many doors on the three sides and Adriana wondered if each led to another room or if they were neat compartments, rooms whole and unto themselves only connected by the walls. She noticed a woman coming from one of the doors on the left. She was tall and distinctly Greek and beautifully put together in a stylish modern black skirt that flared at the knee and a silk blouse that only a woman who hasn't an ounce of fat can wear it was so fitted. She didn't have shoes on her long graceful feet; instead it was silk slippers the same champagne color of her silk blouse.

"Goddess," she said in accented English.

"You've been practicing." Lilika smiled and embraced the woman. "Effemia, this is Adriana. She shall be staying with us for —" Lilika paused to look for the correct phrase or time, "a short time." Adriana nodded and smiled. "Adriana, this is Effemia. She and her family take care of everything in my absence. If you are in need of anything she will be the one to ask." Lilika then addressed Effemia. "We are expecting two more guests in the next couple of days. They will share a room, but put Adriana in the room above my study." Effemia nodded and motioned for Adriana to follow. "It's fine. I need to make a phone call then we can eat if you like or you can rest."

***

Lilika smiled and they ascended the stone stairs. She then went in a door underneath the overhang those stairs led up to. The study was large by anyone's standards with leather couches and a day bed covered with pillows. Three of the walls were lined with built-in bookshelves. The exterior wall, however, had two long vertical windows and a desk that faced the room. It wasn't a Greek room by any stretch of the imagination, filled with all the books and brown leather furniture and dark richly carved wood. On the over-sized desk sat an antique gold and ivory phone that seemed more for the motif than for a workable machine. Lilika sat at the desk and took a deep breath, leaning back into the chair and bringing her linked fingers to her mouth in thought. This was not the turn she wanted things to take. She didn't want to offer immortality to this girl. She was so Christian and American. Not that either one were all that bad, but she had ideas that were conflicting and her need to be daddy's gun toting, straight, all-American girl was throwing a wrench into who she longed to be. Now, thanks to Uncle Ares, she could end up with another heartbreak when it all could have just ended.

She supposed that was the problem with being a war god. No matter how you played the game, destruction was soon to follow and by definition you could never win. Zeus. Why wasn't grandfather stopping him? Ares was obviously working a way to go around Zeus's decree. If Lexia was forced to fight him, then it was she who sought him, not him seeking her. Ares was damn clever sometimes. Luckily there were elements he didn't know about and wasn't able to account for. Lilika looked up and yelled, "Uncle Herc! YO!"

In a red flash of light Hercules appeared. "Lilika! Niece! I've been expecting your call," he said taking a seat on one of the couches in front of the desk. "I know about Ares. I know he is up to something at least. I've been talking to Father about it all day."

Lilika came around the desk and pointed to wine on a table beside the couch. "Yes, well, I can give you the details to give to Grandfather. In a couple of days Lexia can give them to you herself." Lilika handed him a cup of wine. "He pretty much told me his plan. What he didn't know is that I know what he's doing and I also know he'll never finish it as long as I'm alive. When he came to me earlier he said, 'I have three. When it's five I'm doing it.' What he knows is that Lexia knows where some of the pieces are, except she doesn't know the location of all of them, not anymore anyway. This is what he and we should call a win-win. Lexia hunts him down therefore he isn't violating Zeus's decree and he may finally get to wage war on the world. He never got over missing both world wars from last century..." Lilika lowered her voice. "I have one piece."

Hercules took a gulp of wine. "So he doesn't know you have a piece? Is your piece safe? Where is it?" He paused for more wine. "No, keep that to yourself. So the question becomes do we leave the piece where only Lexia knows where it's at or do we retrieve it as a precaution?"

"I wondered the same. It is out in the world. So long as my piece is safe he doesn't pose a threat, but we need all the variables covered in this. He may be bumbling at times but he can be just as clever and ruthless." Lilika sipped her wine.

"I'll speak to Father again. Hopefully he'll do something knowing this." With that he sat his glass down and disappeared in the same red flash he entered with.

***

Lilika resumed her position at the desk. She was about to pick up the phone when there was a knock at the door. Effemia entered with Adriana trailing behind her.

"I have brought your guest and I need to know what to prepare for dinner. I have already sent father to the market to restock the fridge and pantry." She spoke in old Greek that hadn't evolved to the Greek of today. If there was evolution to it, then it was slight at best.

Lilika motioned for Adriana to sit down. "Maybe a simple salad, a small selection of meats with fruit and cheese. I want to hold off on a feast until the others are here," Lilika said in the old Greek. Effemia nodded and smiled to Adriana as she walked out the door.

"So what is for dinner?" Adriana said with a slight laugh.

"I told her a salad, meat, fruit, and cheese. Though what it will turn into is anyone's guess. She is quite the chef." Lilika walked over to a table in front of a book shelf and picked up what looked like a leather bound book and sat it on the couch table in front of Adriana.

"This is something I know you'll want to see and you will be welcome to use." Adriana reached to open the cover of the book only to discover it was a tablet. Lilika smiled. "Fooled you? It actually is a book. Any book you want it to be. An everybook, if you will." Adriana looked at the tablet and back to Lilika. "Say the name of any book and what translation you want or type it and it will pop up in its entirety. It contains every book ever written in any translation. I prefer originals myself because too many things are lost in translation, which brings me to my next question. If you would like I can give you the ability, while you are here, to read any language you want and speak it as well. That way nothing will be lost in translation." Adriana looked at Lilika as if she had grown a second head. She had never been one to pass up learning something that could change her life even if she tended to run away from experiences. She looked at Lilika for a long time. This could mean enlightenment or this could mean death. Like learning the secret of life and being driven mad by it. She knew madness without creation meant death but she also knew this morning she was in a different part of the world, a different state of mind that didn't contain gods and immortals. She inhaled deeply then exhaled. She could use a cigarette and a glass of deep red wine. From nowhere there came a little neat cardboard packet of cigarettes and a silver flip top lighter. She lit one of the little black cigarettes while Lilika poured her a glass of wine.

"I guess if I'm going to do this I should do it all the way," she said before her fear overrode her judgment. Lilika walked over and touched Adriana's forehead with the first two fingers of her left hand. Adriana blinked. "That was it?" she said. She had expected an explosion in her brain.

"Of course it is. What did think that would be, an epiphany? That just gives you a better ability to reach the epiphany." Lilika laughed. It was meant good naturedly but she realized Adriana didn't agree. "I'm sorry, please take the tablet and use it. You now have the ability to read and speak the major ancient languages and the languages that sprung from them."

A few hours passed and Lilika found herself standing outside the door to Adriana's room. She had called Gelesia to see if they were safely on their way and now she was here listening to see if she could glean the girl's actions without actually spying. Eventually, after hearing nothing for a while, she knocked. The door sprung open and revealed a tired looking Adriana.

"I've done nothing but read these last few hours," she said in a voice that was laced with sleep and excitement.

"I can tell. Your eyes are going to swell shut," Lilika said stepping more fully into the room.

Adriana laughed. It was girlish and hung in the air between them. "The reason I disturbed you is it's time to eat. I'm sure you're hungry." Adriana confirmed she was indeed hungry and the pair made for the door. "I thought we could talk some more over dinner. Have you found any interesting texts?"

Adriana decided honesty wasn't key for the moment. "Oh yes. Many." In truth she had been scouring every Greek text she could find about the gods to find out more about the mysterious new god in her life and the story she was telling. All she was able to find was a name and the names of five children; one child who had died and four children that had lived. She found nothing else about the woman in the story. Not even her name. She found no references or even myths of Lilika. She wondered why Lilika denied her access. They sat down at a table in the courtyard behind the fountain. Adriana observed that even though it was a large house it was oddly welcoming. She was at ease here in a way she had never been back home. A stranger in a strange land. She decided that it must be her sense of adventure kicking in.

"Would you like to hear more of the story?"

Chapter 3 Ancient Greece

"Let's see, I left off in *our* story at the second time we had spoken, yes?" The girl sitting across from the goddess shook her head without commenting on the goddess' phrasing. "Ok, well the romance after that burned as bright as the sun. We spent every waking hour together and when she slept I laid next to her watching the rise and fall of her chest. Because she wasn't part of Greek society and her father was not yet an invalid, she had all the time in the world. I showered blessings upon her family. Every day was an adventure for us. We traveled the world that was known, visiting the temples that lay all over Greece. Societies were vastly different at this point in time and not as connected as they would come to be and so there was always much to be learned by her.

"One day would be spent on a southern coast, and by the next morning we were ready for a northern landscape. This was our way for two years. As Adelphie's twentieth birthday approached, I told her I had to go away for a week or so but I would have a grand surprise for her upon my return. She begrudgingly agreed, having grown accustomed to never leaving my side. We had recently been on the southern tip of mainland Greece and I found a secluded piece of coastline with a great cliff on which I was planning to build a house. There was a great city below that I would make my own for us to spend eternity in. It hadn't occurred to me that it could or would be any other way. I left her to build this grand house we are now in. There was a small village nearby that I planned on growing into a beautiful city that would bear Adelphie's name. It took me five days to complete the house by hand and put everything I wanted in order. I needed her to know that I labored over this house and merely didn't *poof* it into existence. I wanted something she would be proud to spend our eternity together in.

"I returned on the 6th night with flowers from the banks of the river that ran by the village. Before I left I started blessing the village with the bounties it would take to grow into a great city. I made the crops larger and more bountiful. I guided traders' ships and caravan routes on their way to Athens through the little village. I made my presence known to what could be priests and what would become rich families that would leave a thousand year legacy. This would be a prosperous place. It was the eve of her birthday and in less than a day from now she would be my immortal lover with the family's permission, which is to say really Zeus and Hera's permission. I was walking on air. She welcomed me with open arms and we made quick work of getting undressed and becoming familiar with one another all over again. I hadn't left her for more than a day in two years and the love we made showed it. The entire night and part of the next day were spent naked. The servants were under orders to leave food at the door and to not disturb us under any circumstance.

"That evening her father had planned an intimate party with her brothers, their wives and children to celebrate Adelphie's birthday. I planned then to inform her of the grand house on the cliff. We arrived a little late to the banquet, what would now be considered fashionably so. The presence of a god usually meant adherence to strict social protocol except for a few instances. Me being part of the family and courting this man's daughter happened to be one of those instances. Therefore, all eyes were on Adelphie and her beauty radiated. Her nieces and nephews were now walking about and they immediately drew her attention away from her admiring family which was increasingly less unusual as time passed. When we took our places at the table her father raised a toast to her twenty summers and to our relationship. Then the feast with succulent trays of roasted beasts, fruits, and wine was served. Ah, the wine was some of the finest in this part of the country and chilled to the perfect temperature by the river bottom.

"Her father was a jovial man who, though his army would follow him to the death, loved to laugh and tell a good joke. Her brothers would never be the leader their father was and all four favored her mother in looks, but they had the same jovial personality and love of laughing. The ones who were married tended to the needs of their wives, who were all beautiful as it seems most Greek women were back then. They suckled their fresh-faced beautiful children then handed them to nurse maids who took them away as the meal was set out. I replaced her oldest brother sitting directly across from her father at the other end of the table. Adelphie sat to my right with her oldest brother, Adrastos, to my left. The other brothers sat on down the line in birth order with those who had wives across from them except Adrastos's wife who sat beside Adelphie. The conversation was light hearted and full of sudden bursts of laughter. Adelphie's father was never one to let conversation lag, whether in the privacy of his home or in public.

"I smiled as I observed this family that let me claim the youngest member as my own. They were a good and strong family. One that I was sure would last until the end of time should there be such a thing. I knew Adelphie and I would make sure it was nurtured and the line survived. We would be the guardians of the children here and the children to come. Maybe this would replace the children she would never be able to have as an immortal. The guardianship of this family could keep her occupied forever if she let it.

"As the evening wound down and night crept upon us, more musicians arrived to serenade us into nightfall. We danced and drank and laughed, never letting on that there was something in the air. A change. Maybe they never sensed it, but I did and I was positive that Adelphie felt it as well. I know now it was the Fates about to change the weave of the fabric that made up this time. The more we danced the more the wine flowed. Adelphie's father saw his chance to have a tête-à-tête with the goddess that he jokingly said stole his daughter.

"You plan on keeping her until her death?" he whispered in my ear, his stale breath mingling with my own as I laughed, admittedly, in his face but he was too drunk to realize.

"No," I said quickly. "I will keep her forever." He gasped and spun me around until we reached the opposite end of the room.

"You have a godly trick for this? She will never grow old?" he said, fear lacing the drunkenness of his voice.

"It is no trick, but no, she will never grow old and she will never die. She will guard your lineage." I threw that last bit in to tip the scale in my favor should he show some odd courage or sudden hatred and try to rip her from me.

"He smiled. He knew my trick. "I love you. You are the one for my daughter, of this I have no doubt. I will worship you all the days of my life, Goddess Lilika."

"I realized this was my cue to whisk her away to our new home. She said her goodbyes and we took our leave. We appeared at the gate of the house. It was then the same design that you saw upon your arrival today. I opened it with a silent push of my mind. The path to the courtyard was lit with so many fireflies there wasn't a shadow to be see. I led her up to the opening of the courtyard where torches burned and all the wooden doors to the house were flung open with torches lighting all the rooms and the porticos around the three sides of the courtyard. She gasped and flung her arms around my neck kissing my face then landing on my lips a kiss that would serve to fuel our passions. I kissed her fervently and lowered her to the ground. She sighed into my mouth as my hands slid up her thighs and pulled her close. She bit into my shoulder when my fingers slipped inside her warm and wet femininity. Deeply inside her, I moaned my own passion as we fell into a motion every lover knows. When the moment finally arrived, I breathed her breath and kissed her from the top of her head to her finger tips and finally down her body until her breath once again became steady.

"As we put our garments as best we could into their proper places once again, she noticed the table at the back of the fountain. I walked over to it and pointed at the apples. 'This is why we are here. I built this house with the explicit intent of us living here for eternity.'

"She walked to where I stood and picked up one of the apples eyeing it with suspicion.

"Hera's?" she said placing it on the table.

"Yes, she and grandfather and your father all have given their blessing. I want you with me forever. I want our time to never end."

"She turned away from me, and her shoulders began to shake. I thought at first she was crying but when she spun around with her finger pointed at my face I knew I was wrong. "You received everyone's blessing?" Her tone was far too even. "Everyone but the one you should have spoken to first. Has it never occurred to you that I want to know what growing old is? I know you haven't the mind to conceive it, but I do. It is just as important as our love of each other."

"I was aghast. This was not supposed to play this way. We are soul mates. We are forever. The transcendence of death is nothing by comparison. She pushed the apple into my chest. I grasped it with my left hand. Her eyes were blazing as she stared directly into mine.

"The fact that I will one day die is why our love is so precious." She said it searching my eyes for an understanding she knew she would never find. I was a god and though I knew humanity was slated to die, it had never happened to one that I loved or been a real part of my life. She would never understand that her death wasn't something that needed to happen and it wasn't why we loved as strongly and permanently as we did. Our souls were two halves of a whole. We were destined to ride this journey out. I knew when she looked away from me that the human and the god could never be. Now wasn't that time. There was nothing I could say. Both our arguments were valid for our species. I let my left hand fall to my side.

"Take me home." The tears in her eyes were glowing in the lamp light. I waved my right hand and she blinked out of the courtyard and into her rooms at her father's house. I lay down on the floor of the courtyard with the apple still in my left hand and stared at the night sky.

"In the days that followed I didn't move. I couldn't. I stared at the sky. I watched Uncle Helios's chariot make its journey. After a time I closed my eyes. My right hand clutched my heart and my left hand held the apple out away from my body. I wanted to die, to find some dark oblivion where I didn't exist, a place where this hadn't happened. Our meeting had been no accident and I couldn't live without her by my side. Determination left me after that. I lay for days and those days turned into weeks. During what could have been the ninth week, Aphrodite showed up. She sat on my stomach with her knees on either side of me. I didn't open my eyes. She yelled my name and slapped me hard across the face. I lay unmoving. She was gone as quick as she came. I'm unsure of how much time passed after this until my brother, Eros, showed up. He lay down beside me with his head propped on his left hand.

"Come on, sis. You're a god. Convince her. She doesn't hate you. Her misery is as great as your misery." He left then, shaking his head I'm sure.

"More time passed and I remained as a statue, fallen over, modeled after some great tragedy. All I could see were her hands and her face. I could smell her all around me. I knew somewhere inside that if I kept my eyes closed and I remained perfectly still then my illusion of her couldn't be broken. She was with me then. We were how I knew we should be. She was doing all those mortal things she loved; taking care of the poor and loving unabashedly on her nieces and nephews. Any number of thoughts about her kept me occupied, kept me still in a place of delusionary contentment. Some time passed and I realized one day that someone was watching me. I sensed them, unable to gauge how long they had been there. Fine, I thought, let whomever this is watch as long as I'm left undisturbed. I couldn't make the presence, only the general direction he or she was sitting. After a time this got the better of me and I became distracted by my curiosity. Then the she spoke. "Open your eyes, child." Mother. Artemis. There was a tone that barred any argument or doing anything but exactly what was demanded. I opened my eyes and inhaled deeply through my mouth. She sat to my right on the edge of the fountain. I sat up letting the apple lay where my hand had been. I was covered in a fine layer of dust. I could tell the seasons had changed but it had been oddly sunny for this part of the country. I shook what dust I could off my clothes and sat at the table waiting for Mother to join me. She

43

appeared wine for us. I drank the honey-colored liquid greedily in large gulps. Even a god's throat can get dry. She waited as I filled and refilled my cup several times. Finally setting it down she nodded her head.

"Go about your life. There are still things to be done. You are still the god you always were." I nodded.

"Aside from that, humans die every day. Humans are reborn every day." She looked at me pointedly. She finished the wine she had poured and left in a golden flash.

"I sat back in my chair. I nodded. She was right. I realized it had been more than two years since I had seen Adelphie. I knew I couldn't spy on her; she would feel my presence, masked or not. Instead, I went to her city's temple. Surely there would be some gossip there I could overhear or some Priestess would have knowledge of her. I heard nothing so I went to another temple with the same result. Finally, after searching a few other temples in the city I called on Mom.

"She appeared in her pink and purple light. "Yes, daughter? I see your Mother came to tell you these dramatics are overrated." She smiled. She knew what I wanted but she wasn't above making me work for it.

"Where has she gone? She mustn't know I search

for her." I sighed, exasperated.

"Mom took a seat. "She doesn't leave her father's house. She came here for a while, but now and for the last year or so she hasn't left his side."

"I knew if the Fates would allow we would be together again one day. I decided then to wait and see. When she left her father's house again, when she was able to leave the gate, that would be when I would come to her. My brain tingled as I plotted this but I ignored the knowledge that was screaming to be let in. I set my mind to this plan and I was going to see it through.

"My routine became mine again, with an eye always on her father's house. I watched her brothers go off to war only to return scarred and two of them never to return at all. Even when they performed their funeral rites she was nowhere to be seen. After a year I began to wonder if my plan was the way to go. I was so blinded by her memory I didn't hear a Priestess screaming for me at a temple just south of Adelphie's.

"I appeared before the woman. "Yes? You must stop this screaming." She was a highborn priestess whom I had never laid eyes on.

"She's…" I held my hand up to stop her. The air crackled around me and there was a pink flash.

"Mom?" I was on my knees suddenly. Someone

had taken away my ability to breathe. The air wouldn't stop buzzing in my ears. Aphrodite yelled my name but I couldn't hear her over the din that surrounded me. The priestess ran from the room. Then, just as quickly as it came it was gone and I was holding my ears for nothing. Aphrodite pulled me to my feet. The tears were already streaming down my face.

"She's gone, Mom."

"I ran from the temple. I ran until I reached the temple of the Fates. I ran through the chambers to where they weave.

"Klotho! Lakhesis! Atropos! What would you have me do now?" They kept at their work never looking at me.

"Artemis has told you what to do."

"I was infuriated. "That means nothing! Her soul may go on but she won't! She cannot! I cannot!"

"On the sisters weaved. "She will change and grow. You will go on. This is the way." They disappeared after that. I was alone in their stone spinning room.

"A hand clamped down on my shoulder and spun me around. It was Artemis. "She'll be reborn. The Fates told you as much. Find her, protect her. Make her yours once again."

Chapter 4 An Interlude: The Story of Lexia and Gelesia. Our Heroes.

"So now you know the story of our beginning." She looked pointedly at Adriana. "I assume you scoured the book for any mention of me or her?" The goddess smiled when Adriana shook her head in the affirmative.

"I didn't remove it to deliberately deceive you. I did it because I wanted you to hear it from me, not some historical account that would inevitably contain inaccuracies. That being said I can tell you of a few other significant moments in our time together or we can go on from here. Lady's choice." The goddess walked around the desk and dropped to her knees in front of Adriana. They had retired to the study after finishing their evening meal.

"Maybe I can study more and you can tell me more. Something tells me this is the safest place to be with the current state of affairs." She smiled down at Lilika.

She would never admit it but the goddess' heart soared at this. Lilika wasn't sure if it was right, she also wasn't sure she could wait another lifetime or if she should. Humanity had already changed so dramatically she wondered what it might do to itself in another one hundred years. Lilika rose to her full height.

"My guests should arrive tomorrow."

"Your guests, how did you meet them? They are gods, too?" Adriana asked, putting down her wine glass.

"No, they aren't gods. Immortals. That's a story in itself. Maybe I can fit it in over dinner," Lilika said winking.

"I met Lexia when she was seventeen. Young, stupid, and angry were the best words to describe her. Her mother and father had died in a plague that ravaged their town so she moved north with her sister and brother-in-law. Then war came and they were killed. Lexia seemed to be fated to die in the street. That's where godly intervention came in, but not by me. She had an anger in her that had attracted Ares. Direct intervention by us is uncommon but not unheard of. Especially with someone who could somehow be of great importance in the future. He fueled her anger and taught her the ways of war. She found her potential and by the time she was twenty, she was leading a band of mercenaries dressed as a man. Eventually she found the army that had killed her sister and brother-in-law. The slaughter was astounding and unnerving. She didn't stop there. She couldn't. A taste for blood is a powerful taste to forget. Throughout this time, over and over I tried to sway her in less direct ways. I knew she could be something better, something different. She had one of the most brilliant minds that had been born up to that particular time. Finally, being indirect wasn't enough and I became more direct. Through this we developed our love-hate relationship. When she was twenty five she met the person that would turn her life around in ways she never allowed me to. It's not the most important part, suffice to say sometimes love, even though not always permanent, can make you question everything.

"When she met Gelesia she was already on her path to enlightenment. She discussed philosophy with anyone who would listen, she travelled and every town she went to the book market was the first stop she made. She still dressed herself as a man then. Since she was stronger and taller than most women she could easily pass. She met Gelesia in one such town when Gelesia had travelled with her father to sell food at the market. For whatever reason, her mother was unable to go and Gelesia, being the eldest of two daughters, was chosen to go with her father. Gelesia will tell you to this day that the minute she saw Lexia she knew her for what she was and realized she was the one for her. Lexia's past didn't matter to Gelesia. She was nearly eighteen and about to be married to a man that had paid her dowry and loved her, but when it came down to it was a son of a bitch who didn't mind hitting anyone who angered him. Also how she would say it now.

"One day, maybe two or three months after they met, Lexia and Gelesia were leaving Athens on horseback. I caught up to Lexia at this time. I had been watching her change but with minimal interest since she had turned from her warmongering. I had a few irons in the fire at that time and needed a break and some fun. I appeared beside them on a horse of my own except I was lying on my back with my head resting on the horse's massive neck. The only acknowledgment was the surprised sigh Gelesia made, but by this time she was learning to take her cues from Lexia even if only half the time and remained silent. Lexia didn't acknowledge me in any way. She kept her eyes forward scanning for danger or any sign of it. We were in a heavily wooded area just entering the countryside. After twenty or so minutes of riding in silence and Gelesia using every bit of her restraint not to speak, Lexia spoke.

"Yes?" she said drawing the word into a lengthy question.

I snickered. "I told you so."

She snorted and turned her gaze back to the road.

"I guess you did." It was possibly the first time she admitted this and while it couldn't be counted as an admittance of her being wrong about something, it did show character growth and I was proud.

"Gelesia could no longer keep quiet. "Hi, I'm Gelesia." She bubbled with the excitement of youth that was the polar opposite of Lexia. I knew I loved her in that moment.

"What do you want, Lilika?" Lexia interrupted our introductions.

Gelesia squealed, "The Goddess? You know a Goddess, Lexia?"

"We aren't friends," Lexia and I spoke in unison.

"Yeah, I see." Gelesia laughed.

"I chose to ignore Lexia's question and turned around on my horse to steer it to Gelesia's side. "So, Gelly, what brings a girl like you to have company like this?"

"Well, I decided that I needed to learn. I want to be a philosopher and a bard. I knew Lexia may be the best way to do that."

"I began to laugh. I couldn't stop myself. The implication was that I was laughing because I thought it was preposterous that anyone could learn from Lexia, which was half true, but I also laughed because Gelesia was pretty well lying through her teeth. She wanted to learn and be a philosopher and all that business, but what she really wanted was Lexia. She was a girl in love.

"I finally quelled my laughter. "Learn from her?" I pointed at Lexia. "What's she going to teach you? How to shine armor while snorting and scowling all at the once?" I finished by doing a very bad impersonation.

Lexia chose that moment to ride ahead.

"Oooh, the Amazon is all pissy."

I was only teasing but Gelly perked up. "Lexia is an Amazon?" she practically yelled.

"She hasn't told you much about herself, has she?" I ignored her question as well. I knew this girl had a thousand questions, none of which she had the courage to ask the other woman. She was only eighteen after all and had lived on a farm. Lexia was a hero to her and someone to be worshipped and loved. Gelesia was lovely though, with her rare golden hair and green eyes. She tended to attract attention in the small towns but blended in perfectly in Athens. The attention irritated Lexia to no end but she continued to 'put up with the girl.' We rode until dusk with Lexia up ahead and Gelesia and I chatting. Well, she chatted and I listened and made the appropriate listening noises at the right moments.

"Lexia circled around to us and declared we

would make camp here for the night a few yards off the path. Lexia sent Gelesia for firewood after tethering the horses down by a small creek.

"What do you want, Lilika?" She was unpacking her saddlebags and her tone showed she was in no mood for banter.

"The last time I had seen her things had not been so tenuous between us and I wondered at what had happened.

"I thought I would pay a visit. See how your journey is going. I'm very proud, you know."

"She put her bag down and looked me in the eye. "No one has said that to you, have they?" I knew they hadn't. Her family was dead and this wasn't a modern age of friends who are family and vice versa. "Why haven't you told that girl anything about yourself?"

"She knows enough." She shot back quickly.

"She really doesn't, Lex. She's a smart girl. I know her quick wit and big mouth has gotten you out of some scrapes." I glared at her but she could see through me or just didn't care that there was an angry goddess in front of her.

"Gotten us into some, too. She's too young. She doesn't need to know all the things I've done, no matter how smart she is. She'll be gone soon anyway. Run back home with that fiancé of hers and be ready to have babies until she dies."

"Lexia, don't make me do the god thing. Play just a little nice. She may surprise you."

"Gelesia was making her way back with the firewood. She laid it on the ground and took a seat beside Lexia. "It feels like rain. Will we be all right here?"

"Lexia was too busy not reacting, which is to say throwing mental daggers at me, to hear Gelesia.

"I spoke up, saying, "No worries, if it rains I'll make sure we don't get wet." I winked at Gelesia who turned to Lexia.

"See, Lexia, not all gods are bad. Lilika offered us shelter."

Lexia smiled sincerely at Gelesia. "So she did."

They decided on fish for dinner and Lexia went to the creek. I knew better than to follow her right then and so stayed with Gelly to help with the fire. "What did you think of Athens? I'm assuming it was your first trip without your father's forced labor."

Her eyes lit up. "Yes, we stayed in this little tavern with all sorts of people. We spoke with philosophers and bards. It was just the kind of experience I longed for." The words spilled out of her as though she hadn't spoken in a month.

"Experience will come, especially travelling with Lexia." She shook her head and stoked our little fire. I wanted to just make the fire brighter and bigger but she insisted on doing it her way. Lexia would be proud was the implication, but I just let it slide and watched her make it.

"I watched the pair of them that night. Even just a few months and they had developed a routine. A balance if you will. It was a graceful dance of preparation. One unrolling the blankets while the other cleaned and built up the fire. They didn't have to speak. They had their parts to play and knew them well. Lexia ignored my bold little smiles. She knew my story well enough to know I delight in those small pleasures and she knew it wasn't something I ever really talked about. When they bedded down for the night, Gelesia closest to the fire with Lexia on the other side of her, I tended the fire and thought about their routine and how long ago it had been for me since that first I loved you. A hundred years to a god can be a blink but not to me. To me it was torture. Living my human life, even with the guarantee of godhood at death, had taught me about time. Before that first life it had been an abstract concept that mortals cherished and feared in the same breath. Now, after living a few human lives I respected and understood time which made nothing easier.

"Lexia was up as the sun crested the horizon.

"Gelesia won't be up for a while," she said as she packed her bed roll.

"Gives you time to think, huh?"

"Looks like you did a fair amount of that yourself." Her tone had changed, and while it wasn't friendly, it wasn't filled with venom, either. "Gelesia appreciated the fire, I'm sure."

"You fishing?" I said smiling evenly.

"We walked to the creek and sat in silence on the bank, Lexia catching the fish and me reclined chewing a blade of grass. It was the first time she wasn't vibing me to death with animosity since I appeared. We came back to the place we were the last time I had seen her. She grappled a few times but in the end caught four good fish that they could use to make a fine breakfast. We watched the sun finish its rise and then she decided Gelesia would most likely be awake by now and we should head back.

"When arrived at camp Gelesia was putting her gear away and then they began their morning routine. They ate in silence. I watched as their body language switched back and forth from easy routine to moments that would come closer to the reality, protector and protected aspect which dominated their time but by no means consumed it.

"Then there were the moments when, without

knowing it, they were a married couple going happily about their routine then something would happen and the spell would be broken. Whether it was a sudden swelling of feelings or an attempt at denial, it was hard to tell — they travelled so fluidly from one to the other. Lexia had her limits but they were a hundred miles in the distance and farther with Gelesia. Finally the spell was completely broken by a need to get back on the road.

***

"The sun was high and Gelesia's stomach hadn't stopped growling for an hour. "You getting hungry?" Lexia asked with a crooked smile after hearing it growl for the umpteenth time in the hour.

"No, we can go on." Gelesia smiled weakly. Lexia shook her head and prepared to go on despite the younger girl's obvious lie.

"Well, I'm ready to take a break. My godly tush is numb and I know the horses are more than ready themselves." Lexia frowned but couldn't disagree about the horses, at least. Gelesia smiled with relief. While Gelesia gathered the cheese and bread, I followed Lexia with the horses to the water.

"It was my turn to scowl and be testy. "The girl is

just looking to keep up with you. Give her a bloody break, would ya?"

"As lunch was being eaten, I did my best to get Lexia to open up just a little. With people of no consequence she could be incredibly graceful and charming. If there was a real chance she could get to know you, she was cold and clammed up tighter than a virgin bride. It was working my nerves but by the end of lunch I had Gelesia in giggles and Lexia cracking a rare smile.

"So you see, Lexia, in the middle of these negotiations with the thugs, didn't realize she had stepped into a huge pile of cow shit and the guys, after catching a whiff, were trying to flee but she kept pulling them back in to the fight. I still wonder what that cow had eaten and how she didn't know she had stepped in it!"

"Lexia came to her own defense. "I thought it was them! Bathing didn't seem to be high on their agenda and they had been on the road a while." She didn't realize what she said so when Gelesia caught my eye we both burst into giggles.

"The rest of the day had been unremarkable until I realized the direction we were heading. "Are you staying on this road, Lex?"

She shook her head yes.

"You know where it ends, right?" Again she shook her head. Still confused I pressed on.

"You're going then?" Another shake of her head. "What are you thinking?"

She was quiet for a moment then sighed. "An apology," she said, steeling her voice.

"They will kill you on the spot. You know they do not forget a grudge."

"Which is why it has to be done." She then rode on ahead. Gelesia had been observing the exchange and Lexia knew she would ask and that I wouldn't lie. She lived with the truth. She didn't need to hear it, especially from me. I was surprised when for a long time Gelesia said nothing and I refused to volunteer the information.

"Anything not to say it out loud to her until finally in a small voice she asked, "What did she do?" I probably should have just said sold some women but that was far too simple an answer. I offered her instead the medium answer. "I know you have heard of the Amazon women. The myth. The legend. All that business. While they are those things, they are also a deeply broken people. So scattered you have to seek a tribe. A few years ago Lexia did just that. She befriended them and ultimately betrayed them. She made herself the queen's consort over a period of months. When the queen had lowered her guard, Lexia's mercenaries swooped in and made a quick buck by selling the women, including the queen's sister." I sighed. I hated this story. A million times I'd wanted to intervene. Mother had wanted to intervene. The Fates wouldn't allow it. Mother raved but the Fates were deaf to her screams. Gelesia nodded either in understanding or absolute ignorance; at the time I was unsure which.

"We rode until nightfall and neither woman spoke again. Their routine played out in silence but it was a louder silence than before. We were still a week's ride at the pace we were traveling. The instant we entered Amazon territory, Lexia would be fighting a war alone. She would lose, and with the confidence of an egomaniac, she was marching to her death. All of this in the name of an apology that shouldn't be made. A person can't just apologize for selling people.

"After Gelesia had fallen asleep, Lexia moved over to where I sat. "I need you to keep her here and keep her safe."

"I looked at her for a long moment, staring into her eyes. I sighed and sobered. "I can't. I'm leaving. I refuse to watch your suicide mission. You know this isn't right. You are trying to take the easy way out."

"She looked at her hands then to the fire. I had cut her with my words and she knew I was right, but she also knew the crushing guilt and it was the heavier burden. Lex always knew when to leave. I popped out after that, leaving her at the fire and to listen to Gelesia's light snores alone. I went straight to the Amazon village. I couldn't let her die. I knew she had too much left to do. I spent the night whispering in the queen's ear and then in the morning I spoke to her directly. I spent five days by her side trying to seal the wound and quell the anger, if just a little.

"On that sixth day after my arrival as the sun rose, word came that two women had arrived in Amazon territory on horseback. I stood invisibly at the queen's side only revealing myself to Gelesia as they approached. I could smell the girl's fear. I put my finger to my lips and winked. She eased her posture but kept a grip around Lexia's waist. At some point they had downsized to one horse. I figured they had sold the other to make a hasty getaway easier for Gelesia. She rode slowly toward the queen who was seated at a makeshift throne built for the occasion. Even on the horse, Lexia had to look up to meet the queen's gaze but only a little. I hated to deceive her like this and make her sweat it out, but she deserved this and I loved to watch her live uninterrupted. She stopped in front of the queen and eased off the horse signaling for Gelesia to stay on. She didn't waste any time bowing immediately.

"I've come to beg for your forgiveness." Doing this, asking for this, nearly drained her but she put her pride away and managed. Gelesia never took her eyes off Lexia. Without revealing myself to anyone but Gelesia and the queen, I walked over and slid up on the horse behind her.

"It's alright. I've spent these last five days with the queen. She has agreed to let Lexia live but only that." Gelesia leaned into me. Her breath became even but she was still gripped with fear.

"The queen remained silent, having pride of her own to swallow. In truth, she had every right to take Lexia's life but she was forced to honor me and to honor the Fates. Calmly the queen approached Lexia.

"Stand. Choose a weapon." The queen wasn't going to kill her, but she did plan to beat the hell out of her.

"Lexia stood. "I will not fight. Kill me if you will." The queen chose that moment to strike Lexia across the face. As she went to grab her cheek another blow was landed on her chest. The queen could hit Lexia all day and she would still be on her feet. I only hoped Lexia would fall before the queen did beat on her all day. Blow after blow she stood there. Blood trickled from her nose and cuts on her mouth and cheeks. Bruises started to appear on her arms and around her face. Finally, after what felt like an eternity of restraining Gelesia, Lexia fell to her knees. I couldn't tell if she had seen and heard Gelesia or if she had truly been beaten, but I breathed out the breath I hadn't realized I was holding. The queen stopped and called for her attendants to help Lexia to her personal bathing hut. I told Gelesia to follow them and I had the horse put in the stable then followed the queen to her hut.

"Well, you didn't kill her." She wouldn't look at me.

"I could barely keep from it, Goddess. She may stay until she is healed enough to leave. Alive, but unforgiven." She shook her head and began to cry. "You shall be blessed twice for this," I said then left to go to Lexia and Gelesia.

"I went to the hut where the girls were being attended. I wanted to personally tell them they could stay until Lexia's wounds were healed enough for her to travel. Lexia shook her head. I think she was afraid her voice would betray her pain if she spoke. When they were shown to the hut they would be staying in I took my leave. I knew this experience would bond them in an unbreakable way. Lexia didn't put up an argument when Gelesia assisted in cleaning her wounds nor did she when the younger woman assisted her with food and drink. The queen may have broken the wall down just enough for Gelesia to climb it a little higher and peak over the top.

"When I left them, I stayed away as far as they knew. I was after all still following Adelphie's soul, but I kept an ear open in case Lexia decided to do something stupid, again. Turns out I should have stayed by their sides because love may have grown in their hearts but it did nothing to make them speak it. They were so close a casual observer would have said they were lovers but they kept it tucked away like rage in the pit of their stomachs.

"Eventually, I caught up to them in Antioch. Why they chose to travel that far to the east baffled me, but a quest is a quest. I came upon them in a tavern that wasn't terribly shabby, seated at a table in the back of the room. They were sharing a light dinner mainly because most of their money went for a room and a hot bath. I watched to see where they were with each other. Lexia sat with her back to the wall and Gelesia to her left.

"The care Lexia took in choosing a table and making sure Gelly had what she needed before her own meal alone spoke volumes. I got a little closer to inspect Gelly. She had lost her childhood chubbiness and was becoming a beauty in her own right. They ate mostly in silence, worn out from the day's travel and nearly ready to retire to the room they had purchased. I stopped a serving girl and ordered more food to be brought over to their table immediately should they choose to leave. When the food was brought I appeared in the seat opposite Gelly.

"Looks delish!" I said.

Gelesia squealed and yelped, "Where have you been in so long?"

"I smiled and picked up a piece of meat on a bone waving it dramatically. "Around. I had stuff and people to attend to." I took a bite of the meat. "Guys, dig in. I can hear your stomachs and they are calling for more than the morsels you fed them."

"As they picked up food and began to eat, Gelesia called me out. 'You just disappeared.' She sounded hurt but her inflection said she understood. I guessed that Lexia had informed her of my personal tragedy, or mission, depending on the day and point of view.

I turned to Lexia. "Your wounds healed quite nicely. No lasting damage or limp?" She shook her head in the negative.

"So how is Antioch?" I asked conversationally even though their attention had gone fully to the plates in front of them. "That well?" I said to myself.

"Gelesia laughed and with a swallow of wine said, "Yes, it's well. We haven't been here but these last few hours. It's amazing here from what we've seen."

"Well, love birds, I think first thing tomorrow you need to check out the book shops then settle in and listen to the philosophers." I smiled at them. Lexia was shooting me daggers and I was sure a growl was going to erupt from her throat at any moment. Gelesia giggled and had the sense to blush and look away.

"Oh, just admit it. It's been a damn year and you skirt around each other like young people. You girls aren't getting any younger." I had the good sense of my own to disappear after saying that. I watched from the bar. I stayed far enough away so as not to be conspicuous and with the ears of a god I heard Gelesia say, "She's right you know. I'm in love with you. You are in love with me. Don't give me silence on this, Lex. Our feelings aren't going to change and you know it." She got up and went to the room they were sharing.

"I sent an invisible smack to the back of Lexia's head. She glared but got the message and followed the girl. I drank my cup of wine in silence. Sometimes it does take a less than subtle push.

"Lilika sighed and looked at Adriana's enraptured

expression. She wondered if this was a wise story to tell Adriana or if she should have let her friends tell their own story.

***

Adriana looked confused at the turn of emotions but merely stood, picking up her glass of wine. Before she turned to walk out, Lilika spoke up. "I was only going to say we will have a large feast so study up. The next few days a lot is going to happen and not all of it will be pleasant."

Adriana exited the library carrying the bottle of wine with her. She turned and winked at Lilika before closing the door.

Lilika walked back around her desk turning her chair to look into the night that had fallen during their after dinner discussion. A light rain began to fall causing the fireflies to take shelter. The goddess smiled. The calm before the storm was presenting itself at this moment. She laced her fingers making a steeple of her index fingers and bringing them to her lips. She had heard a tale that this action was a sign of a wise person. Lilika didn't know if it was true, but she found it comforting just the same.

Chapter 5 Arrival

The next morning, Adriana found Lilika's study locked and breakfast arrived at her room. The woman who brought it said nothing, and while pleasant enough, didn't give away any detail of the goddess' whereabouts. The girl ate on autopilot, still involved in reading the ancient stories.

Lilika on the other hand was busy in the village that lay in the valley below the house. She was bestowing blessings that in the back of her mind she was afraid she would never get to bestow again.

If for some unknown reason Ares' plan came to fruition, it would be a long struggle for earth and its people. She just hoped that her people, the people in this village, were strong enough to live without her should it come to that. After visiting the surrounding farms, Lilika headed straight to the temple. She laughed at this action. All this time and she had never physically come into the temple. She stood on the altar without a second thought. "All this reminiscing," she whispered out loud.

The people of the town had built the temple and she listened from afar but could never venture in. She couldn't bear the smells, the gifts, and the priestesses flittering around. It was the last Greek temple now. All the gods knew it, but Aphrodite was the only god to actually enter it. She said there was no reason for all those gifts to just sit there unloved. Even if she only got the pearls or other expensive trinkets while completely neglecting the blessing bit telling Lilika these were her people and her blessings to give away.

Lilika was surprised with the beauty of the temple and how well kept it was to be so ancient. She wondered if all the ruins could still be thriving if humanity hadn't moved on and neglected those beautiful places. She knew it had taken years for the villagers to build the temple but she never knew why. The dedication astounded her. She had always been proud of her town but now she stood in awe. Even if the people who built it were long dead, their descendants were still here thriving and maintaining this beautiful place along with others in the village. The town, as hidden as it is from the world outside, still housed many modern conveniences and ways.

The temple was no exception. There was a mish-mash of ancient and modern instruments in the corner behind the giant altar. Lilika picked up a violin and eyeballed it. She tucked it under her chin and fingered the strings for a moment then began playing. She hadn't picked up an instrument since the last time she saw Gelly. Frantically she played a few lines of Beethoven not realizing she had drawn the attention of the priestesses. The more she played the more frantic the playing became. She swayed to and fro beginning to float with her eyes closed. Her playing became a catharsis, releasing all that had built up in the last couple of days.

With an audible pop of the strings breaking, Lilika was forced to abandon her playing and floated back to the floor. She then noticed the two spying priestesses cowering in the doorway.

They gasped and began to cry.

"We are sorry!" they cried out in unison.

Lilika raised her hand for silence. The women whimpered but halted their apologies. She put the violin down and walked slowly toward the women. Lilika put her hand to each woman's cheek. "I bestow a lifetime of blessings to you and your house," she said to each woman. Lilika then disappeared leaving the priestesses in a swoon smiling in the doorway.

The sun was fully in the sky now and the stalls in the market were open. Lilika walked invisibly through the market admiring the flurry of activity that surrounded her. She let the noise invade her ears drowning out the thoughts, drowning out Ares and Adriana. Her life was a sudden supernatural soap opera. Ridiculous and completely ordinary except for the gods and immortals. At least she wasn't in the restrictive human skin.

It was past noon when Lilika had blessed the town for what could be the final time and she started her way back to her own home. Lilika was strolling, enjoying the winding dirt road and the feel of the leather reins of her blonde mare in her hands. As she approached her gate she saw the back of two familiar heads meandering up to the house as well.

Lilika whistled causing both heads to whip around in unison. The smaller woman flashed a brilliant smile. The taller, dark haired woman merely stared then extended her hand as Lilika approached.

"Hello, old friend," Lexia said finally giving a small smile.

"It's good to see you, Lexia," the goddess said then turned to the smiling blonde, grabbing her into a rodeo hug. They spun around and laughed kissing each other on the cheek.

"Gelly, how have you been? Come inside, both of you. There is a feast tonight and then we can get down to why I have called you here." The goddess opened the heavy gate letting the two women in before locking it behind her.

"That was a little dramatic," Lexia said, a little skeptical of the goddess's motivations.

"It is merely for peace of mind, and besides it looks pretty." The goddess winked.

Lilika and the two women walked up the small hill and to the main courtyard. There was a flurry of activity leading from the kitchen. A large table had been placed at the end of the courtyard behind the fountain, where women were placing layers of tablecloths and place settings. A door above their heads on the right opened and a dark haired young woman flew down the steps.

"I thought you had left or been captured!"

The girl came to a halt in front of the goddess, suddenly realizing there was a woman on either side of her. The smaller blonde was standing very close holding Lilika's hand.

"Adrianna, this is Lexia." She motioned to the taller woman with the hand that wasn't being held hostage by the small blonde.

"And this," she wrapped her arms around Gelesia, "this is Gelesia, the only other woman to have my heart."

They all laughed as Lexia said, "And dancing shoes."

Adrianna shook her head in the affirmative.

"It is nice to meet you both."

"But to answer your question, I was in town taking care of some last minute business."

As the women spoke, another smaller table was brought out along with wine and fresh fruits. Lilika motioned for everyone to sit as glasses of wine were poured. Lilika asked one of the women to take Lexia and Gelesia's luggage to another guest room.

"Unless you prefer to sleep in the rooftop garden underneath the stars, of course." The goddess smiled sweetly at Lexia.

***

Lexia and Gelesia retired to their room to rest before the meal that evening. Adriana took this opportunity to ask Lilika about the two women, in particular her omitted closeness to the small blonde. She followed Lilika to her study and sat down on the leather couch facing the study with the row of books behind it. She hadn't sat on this couch before, always opting for the one by the fireplace. She was silently berating herself for not looking up stories about these women. They were both very beautiful and not at all what Adrianna had pictured. She had imagined Lexia to be a shorter version of Lilika; instead she seemed to take up the entire room. Adriana was sure that was mostly her demeanor and not the fact that she was six feet tall with a surfer's build. Gelesia was sweet as apple pie and couldn't have been more than five feet and four...why would she have Lilika's heart is what kept flashing through her mind. How did that happen with the tall imposing companion around?

Lilika's voice pulled Adriana out of her reverie.

"They aren't what you expected, are they?" Lilika asked taking a seat at her desk. The girl smiled and shook her head.

"I didn't realize you and Gelesia were so close." She tried to sound confused or casual, not accusatory.

"Oh yes, if ever I had a bosom friend it is that little woman. It is after all my fault they are immortal. Well, I say fault but meddling is really the word." Lilika laughed to herself.

Adriana let out a sigh of relief. The thought of competition suddenly frightened her which only added to her confusion about the situation in which she currently found herself. Everything she knew to be true turned out to be false but still seemed to be true. Her lack of comprehension made her want to run and hide. Forget the whole situation existed. Still she was stuck and too much of a coward to ask to go home. Aside from not being safe, who knew if running away would dispel all this knowledge. Knowledge that felt familiar—she knew all of this, but somehow didn't. Without another word she went to the rooftop garden to lay in the shade of the trees. She plopped down on the hammock and closed her eyes. She was ready to cry. Confusion was not her friend. She knew there was a choice to be made and she needed to have all the knowledge before she could begin to conceptualize what was actually happening in front of her. She was about to drift off into a fitful nap when footsteps caused her to snap back to reality.

"Hello." The woman's voice wasn't overly friendly but had a curt politeness to it. Adriana sat up.

"Hello in return." She smiled at Lexia.

Lexia took the chair by the hammock and looked at the girl.

"So you are the latest incarnation." It was a direct statement but would have been a question if spoken by anyone else. Adriana gave the affirmative nod.

"You were there when Ares showed up." Another question posing as a statement.

"Yes, we were at a park saying what we thought was goodbye." The tall woman acknowledged Adriana's words with what sounded like a grunt.

"I'm sure we will see the bastard again soon. Are

you staying?"

Finally, Adriana thought, an actual question.

"I suppose. I don't really know what is happening. It has all happened so quickly. A sudden adventure that has me questioning everything my life was built upon." The words flooded out like water. She wished immediately for the ability to pull them back in.

"You'll know what is right. Maybe it's time." The tall woman walked away before the girl could say more. She closed her eyes and began to breathe evenly, hoping to recapture her sleep state.

She awoke some time later to music she had never heard. Adriana couldn't identify the instruments, but it was decidedly upbeat and festive. She was going to freshen up before dinner, and as she passed she looked over the ledge to see Lexia sitting with a large man with hair to his shoulders. They were laughing at something she had said. She looked around for Lilika and Gelesia upon spotting an old record player which served as the source of the music. She saw the pair nearby involved in a dance. They spun around each other in time to the music never looking away from the each other's eyes. The two women were intensely involved in the movements, drawing close to one another then parting to spin again. Adriana had never seen a dance that looked so intimate without a fair amount of grinding and a heavy backbeat. This was something new altogether that was actually very old. Suddenly she blushed and turned to go prepare for dinner.

For their part, Lilika and Gelesia were reminiscing in their favorite way. Dance. Lilika had created many records of ancient music for the occasion and they were all dressed in the old ways. Colorful tunics with colorful accents and threads were the preferred apparel for the feast. Lilika was dressed in her preferred color of aqua with her red cape thrown over a chair during a particularly sultry dance move.

Gelesia was wearing her gray tunic with green accents that matched her green eyes. They spun around each other, remembering the first time they had performed it at a temple festival.

Lexia and Hercules sat telling old war stories and discussing the merits of fallen enemies, both avoiding the subject that would have to be the topic for dinner. Lexia was wearing her blue tunic which was her preferred color since she had seen it in a village painting. Hercules was in his usual white with silver accents. He had long ago sworn off gold because of a strong distaste for the color yellow.

Lexia and Hercules were just about to join the

dance when Adriana came down the stone stairs. She looked out of place and felt it. Everyone smiled and they took seats on either side of the table. Lilika sent Effemia to bring the food.

"So we begin," Lilika said with a certain amount of dread. She hated being backed into a corner and saving the world was not her idea of a good time. She preferred books, wine, women, and dancing.

Hercules turned to Lexia." Is there anyone who knows where the hidden piece is?"

"No one alive," she said somberly. "Still, we should fetch it, preferably right after it was placed. Can we reach through time?" she asked looking back and forth between Hercules and Lilika.

"We can't. It would give us away to use such power. The only reason we can fetch it at all is because Ares can't go where Lexia treads, and even then it is a risk."

Lexia spoke up. "It is under water now. On horseback it will take a few days unless we want to risk inquiry by Poseidon." She reached for a wine bottle. This wasn't what she wanted to do but the bastard that was Ares wouldn't stop unless forced to.

"We could ride tomorrow. I can have them ready the horses." Lilika's joy from the dance had officially ended. Everyone nodded in agreement except Adriana who sat quietly chewing on fruit she had never heard of.

"You will be safest here, Adriana." Lilika smiled. Best laid plans and all that she thought.

"You can continue to read and learn. Not to mention drink my delicious wine," she said holding up her glass.

"Hear! Hear!" The gathering echoed.

The meal continued with conversation ranging from the motives of Ares, which everyone agreed were less than pure, to stories of times and dances past. Eventually Gelesia and Lilika resumed their dancing because neither could resist a good beat. They danced well into the night, Effemia and her father lighting torches so the group could see the entire courtyard as though it were daylight. The others would dance if beckoned, but it was Gelesia and Lilika who never stopped unless for wine.

Around three in the morning Hercules excused himself and left for home. Lexia found herself carrying Adriana to her room. She had drank and stared at the dancers until her wine soaked mind had faded into sleep. Gelesia and Lilika continued to dance, only stopping as the sky became streaked in purples and oranges of the oncoming sunrise.

"We haven't danced all night since the moon ceremonies," Lilika said, lying down in the hammock on the garden rooftop making room for

Gelesia as she spoke.

"Yes, now those were parties. All those women bodies painted and dancing," she said, yawning and lying across the goddess with her head on Lilika's shoulder.

"Sleep now," said the goddess, drifting off into a rare wine-induced sleep with her arms around the blonde.

***

Mid-morning found Adriana and Lexia seeking food, water, and their companions. When after breakfast neither had shown, Lexia said she would tend to the horses and get readied what they would need for the journey.

Adriana had decided to retire to the rooftop to read. She stopped short, spying the sleeping immortals. They were facing each other in a bundle of arms and legs. Before she could turn to go, Lilika stirred and caught the look of surprise and confliction on the girl's face. She unwrapped herself from the sleeping woman and grabbed Adriana by the hand.

"Why are you harmed?" the goddess asked, not understanding and barely able to resist reading her mind.

"I'm not sure," the girl said dropping her head. "She is your best friend after all." She smiled.

"I will be here, hopefully with a grand understanding, when you return." She spoke with more confidence than she felt.

Chapter 6 Travel

The day was spent in preparation for the journey up the coastline. Hercules had planned to stay at the house, if only to make sure Ares didn't make a special guest appearance. He was looking forward to a break. He had been pleading with his father to put an end to this madness, but Zeus dismissed the idea that Ares would ever be successful.

For their part Lilika, Gelesia, and Lexia were almost giddy for the journey. They agreed it had been at least 1,984 years since they had traveled the Greek countryside together, give or take a decade or two. Two blonde palominos and a beautiful gray Arabian were at the gates as they met to say goodbye to Hercules and Adriana.

"Adriana, Uncle Herc will not let anything happen here." As she was finishing her sentence a large black dog with blue eyes trotted up to them.

"Amynta! You naughty hound. Where have you been?" Lilika was nearly hysterical as the dog stood on her back legs placing a paw on her shoulders.

"Now, now, quiet. I have been playing spy," the dog said saucily then put her paws back on the dirt. "Go now. My wanderings can wait," she said sauntering through the gates.

As the giant dog trotted off, Adriana fainted.

Hercules caught and held her aloft. Lilika walked over and lightly slapped the girl on the face. She blinked and slowly regained consciousness. Lilika laughed along with the rest of the group.

"Did… did I...pass out?" she mumbled, finding her feet on the ground.

"Yes," the goddess whispered putting an arm around her, "you are fine. It was only my dog. She talks, yes, but it is ok." Lilika pushed her bangs out of her face and stroked her cheek looking deeply into her eyes. Hercules cleared his throat and set Adriana down.

"You'll be fine." She smiled when the girl smiled. They snickered and squeezed each other tightly. Adriana realized this was among many things she was going to ponder and possibly ask Hercules. He seemed approachable. Imposing by his sheer size, but he had a kind face that was rarely without a smile.

The three women mounted their horses and, waving their final goodbyes, headed northwest toward different cliffs.

***

"How do you see this going?" Lexia asked after an hour of silence. Each woman had been contemplating the ending. Lexia wondered if gods

83

were weaker these days without all the build-up of the worshipers. Gelesia wondered about the merits of spending eternity chopped up into little pieces which she feared was their fate. Lilika just wanted this mess over and couldn't figure out the best way to accomplish it. If Ares' plan to bring back any evil man or monster with this machine succeeded, then who knew what this world would become.

An idea was forming in Lilika's head and the more it formed the more fearful she became. She knew death was imminent; it was only a matter of whose. She held her face to the sunshine as her idea took full form. No matter how much knowledge filled the little American reincarnation's head, she would never be her lost love. She needed to go home and live out her natural life. A tear rolled down Lilika's cheek. She screamed Adelphie's name inside her mind, but it left her lips as less than a whisper.

She traveled back through her mind, closing around her golden times. The ancient days. Greece. A time the ancients called ancient. Adelphie was there staring at the water in her father's fountain. Her hair was up in a bun with brown curls falling around her face. She looked up and saw Lilika watching her. A smile took over her face and she opened her arms.

Lilika seemed to float into her arms, burying her

face in Adelphie's neck. She breathed deeply. Everything about Adelphie was perfect in her memory. The softness of her flesh, the way her hairs tickled just everything. Ears, nose, face. Lilika smiled to contain the tears.

She blinked. The sun had gone behind the clouds. The tears on her face dried. Her idea would soon be actions. She turned to face her companions and smiled. "I think it is going to fly like a lead balloon." She winked.

They rode on in silence until Gelesia started to giggle. She giggled until it became a full laugh. On and on she laughed. Finally she snorted and attempted to control her laughter.

"Really, Gelly?"

"We have done this before," she said.

"Many times," Lexia said, only slightly annoyed at being suddenly yanked out of her reverie.

"No, I mean we have traveled this exact road. On horseback. On a *mission*," Gelly said, putting an air of flippancy in the last sentence.

Lexia and Lilika looked at each other wondering how a road could last that long and neither recalling the exact incident to which she referred.

Gelly sighed. "It was after the apple incident. Well after, in fact. We weren't on a mission so much as dressed as men once again to keep safe because things had taken quite a turn."

Lexia shook her head. "After the fall. When everyone was coming together but being torn irrevocably apart."

"Ah, Christianity." Lilika shook her head.

They all laughed. The world had always found a way to eat us a whole. One concept they agreed upon. Riding on in amiable silence it became clear their journey wasn't just physical. Not only had the people changed themselves, they had changed the landscape. People moved mountains for progress. They let mountains crush them when progress seemed impossible.

After stopping to feed the beast that was Gelly's stomach, they rode on until the horses were in need of a break. Lilika cloaked their camp and they settled down next to a roaring fire for the evening. Gelesia was reading out loud to Lilika and Lexia as Lexia looked over her small array of weapons. She worried that they may actually be needed. She hated the idea that Ares was doing all of this to get to her. She loved her life and she loved Gelesia. She wondered if she killed him would he stay dead? Could he stay dead now that the gods didn't have the power they once possessed? She had stabbed Lilika on a couple of occasions and it never took. Getting to this piece of the machine was going to be a picnic compared to the lives-long struggle of keeping Ares from it. Only a select few knew where it was and she was the only one left alive. All their friends had died so long ago it seemed like they were just stories they told themselves when reminiscing. She smiled sadly and began to listen to Gelly intently.

She was reading from a popular modern writer who told funny and clever lies to make a story. She liked this. She needed lighthearted in this moment. Lilika smiled at her and she returned the smile meaning it with her whole heart. Lilika was someone she'd spent a lot of time hating and then loving and then hating. She had to admit, though, that the goddess would walk through fire to save them and was the least selfish of any god she had met. She still remembered the venom she had had for her after she assisted Gelesia in fooling her into immortality. She saw it all for the best now and wouldn't trade a second of it, but right after she could have killed Lilika and tried stabbing her. She succeeded with the stabbing, just not with the killing. Her biggest regret for a long time.

How Gelesia had pleaded with her that it was for the best, how now they would never be apart. Except they *were* apart. Maybe only for one hundred years but they were definitely apart. She went farther to the north than anyone at the time had been while Gelesia spent her time in and out of the company of Lilika at her mansion. It was a time she didn't care to revisit. Those northern plains were cold and remained still mostly unexplored by man to this day. She only knew a fraction of the secrets they held and the beauty they displayed. On foot and in ancient garb it was no easy trek. It was cold enough to freeze her bitterness at immortality, and when she headed south again, she was truly reborn. Her bitterness had melted as the climes got warmer. She was warm and happy now. Happier than she had been in millennia and even though the situation was dire, that was part of the happiness. An excuse for adventure and danger. It was suddenly a beautiful life.

***

Back at Lilika's ancient mansion Adriana and Hercules were sharing an afternoon meal. Chilled wine with cheese and some kind of roasted meat that Adriana decided was better left to being unnamed. She wondered just how she should start her questions or if she should even ask them at all. After all, this could be considered praying to a false god but maybe that was semantics. She knew that she wasn't this ancient woman that Lilika so loved, even if she did harbor the woman's soul, but she couldn't deny the nagging ache she'd felt since she had met her. Not just the god but the person the god was. Should she say yes? Could she be a person with all this knowledge? The irony was once again crashing around her that she had searched her entire adult life and now she had answers that she couldn't reconcile with her faith.

She looked at Hercules. He had a small smile at the corners of his mouth, just a ghost of a smile, she thought, like he knew her secret pain. His face was open which filled her with a sudden courage just as the wine was working on her brain. Adriana took a deep breath and upon exhaling said "So, you know this whole game. What does she want from me exactly? I can't be that ancient woman she lost." She poured another glass of the deep red wine.

Hercules nodded. "She doesn't expect you to be. She wanted only to get to know you, but with my brother's meddling I am afraid the situation got quite out of hand."

"Out of hand?" Adriana nearly shouted.

"Yes," Hercules said patiently, "out of hand. She wouldn't have forced this upon you for all the love in the world. She never would have told you any of it, if I am honest. You would have only ever seen the human friend." He sighed. He did not like this turn of events. This girl was full of presumption and really had a naïveté that left a bad taste and made him fear for Lilika.

"What do you mean? She doesn't see me as her ancient love and won't make me the offer of immortality?" Adriana was defeated. This wasn't the way she saw this conversation going. She didn't like the implication that she would no longer have a choice in the matter. This was her life so she should have a modicum of control.

"No, I am merely saying that you don't believe this and you never got to know her without all of these battle plans in the way. She would never expect you to change your life on the assumption it may be great. Ultimately, this isn't about who has the power but it is about the most unpredictable thing on the planet: Love."

Adriana shook her head. This giant man had a point. She only knew these as stories and only in a roughened, quick-paced fashion. While Hercules may not have given her an answer, he had added more logical questions or at the very least a more logical line of thought. Adriana took a bite of cheese, trying to swallow her pain with the bite unsuccessfully.

"So I should what? Just go back to the States and let her wipe my slate clean on all of this?"

"Or beg her to let you keep your memories so you

can marinate in them and maybe come out having learned something about not only yourself, but this life that you are leading." He stared into her eyes to drive his point home. "Even if you can't be together now maybe on the next go round you will have a better chance with each other."

 She liked that idea. She had to admit not just a small part of that was the fact that she wouldn't have her memories wiped. After their meal they decided to go in to the village. It was a steep walk made steeper by being on horseback, but Adriana decided a little adventure was in order. It may take her mind of off all this doom and gloom. When they passed through the entrance, they were bombarded with people heading back to the market after their own meals and afternoon rests. Finding a stable was easy enough and they took to the market on foot. There were beautiful carpets of all shades and designs at every turn. Next they came to the book sellers which also sold paper and ink. Adriana was positive she had never seen so many kinds of paper in one place. Leather bound books, scrolls, loose paper, and what looked like a modern three ring binder but instead of plastic and metal it was tied with small leather straps at two, three, and sometimes four spots depending on the amount of paper it held. She realized she had no money but the man in the stall had a nose for her and told her to pick what she liked as it would honor the goddess. She began to modestly refuse but then Hercules pointed out that it was an insult and to take what was offered, if only so she didn't appear ungrateful. She relented and picked a beautiful bound book that contained some of Ovid's lesser known works, a beautiful fountain pen, and a blank set of papers bound with the little leather straps in three places and intricately painted little carvings in the leather itself. She was almost positive the little figures around the cover were of the Olympian Pantheon but didn't ask for conformation. They moved on then to the food sellers. Some of the fruits and vegetables looked delicious even if they were unfamiliar to her. Hercules graciously told her what she couldn't identify and showed her that she had eaten some of the foods at the feast back at the mansion. After sampling some of the raw foods, they skipped the meat market and went to the wine sellers.

Adriana wanted to browse the selections and maybe get a free sample or two. She was feeling more at ease in Hercules' company and he was very companionable so she wondered if maybe she should restart the discussion they had been having at lunch.

"Do you think it is fair? What she does, I mean,

traveling through lifetimes in pursuit of this one soul?" She looked at his face in earnest.

"Fair? I figure nothing is fair. Was it fair what you did so long ago? You abandoned her first, you know? She has been fighting that ever since. So I don't think fair can really be used here. There isn't room for it."

"But *I* didn't abandon her. It may have been the woman who housed my soul, but it wasn't me!" She kept her voice even but relayed the anxiety she felt nonetheless. "Look, I'm not trying to make light of the situation. I can understand the trauma, but why couldn't she respect the woman's decision and just let go?"

"Could you?" he said and walked up ahead of her taking a seat at an outdoor pub. He motioned for wine and bread with olive oil and spices. Adriana came up to him and took a seat. She wanted to say 'that's fair' but knew it wasn't. He was right. Nothing about any of this had been fair. She would like to kick that woman in the pants or toga or whatever they wore she thought bitterly. They nibbled on bread in silence, watching people around them come and go. She wondered how this village hadn't become a metropolis since it had existed since ancient times. It just didn't seem possible.

Hercules spoke up. "The people here live longer lives. They find fulfillment not just in getting married and having a family, but in other areas like art, music, philosophy, or their work. That is why there is no population boom."

Adriana shook her head as if that wasn't a completely foreign concept. She had after all grown up under the *be fruitful and multiply* mentality. They continued to nibble their bread until he asked if she were ready to leave. This was only day one of a possible week of waiting and he cautioned they shouldn't see it all in one go. She agreed and they took off for the stables to ride back to the mansion. The sun was beginning to set and the sky was red and purple as they reached the gate to the house. Adriana asked if he minded her eating in her room as she had more reading she wanted to do and maybe some writing as well. Hercules thought that was a wonderful idea and retired himself to the training room on the other side of the courtyard above the kitchen. Each enjoying the evening in their separate ways.

Chapter 7 Fetch

The women approached the cliff from the south, their horses glad to be finished with this leg of the journey. Tying the reins to some trees with plenty of grass nearby, the women approached the edge of the cliff face on foot. All three were excited to get this over with and return to the relative safety of the mansion. While the journey had been an exciting time in all the reliving and reminiscing, it was also a dangerous game that Ares had involved them in and all three were ready to get this done.

"So this cave, how did you get to it originally?" Lilika said looking over the edge. The sun was shining on the water and she hoped that Hercules had gotten Great Uncle Poseidon's wife, Amphitrite, to agree to create a distraction for the great god of the sea.

"Well, I had to swim up to it then climb the face of the cliff. It appears as though the water has risen some since then," Lexia said as she surveyed the rocks for any clue as to how much the water had risen.

"You think?" Gelesia snorted. Lexia gave her a look that said I want you to shut up but I love you.

"I guess I will be swimming into it this time." With that, she pulled off her clothes leaving only a wet suit on and jumped over the edge and into the murkiness of the crashing ocean water. Lexia swam for some time, feeling along the rock for any sign of an opening. She nearly panicked thinking that maybe it had disappeared and she would be looking forever. After all, she couldn't exactly drown. Deeper and deeper she went until the sun's light was a mere suggestion above her head. It occurred to her that she wouldn't be able to see in the cave and should have brought a light source or just let Lilika come down and find the urn. Finally, after what she was pretty sure was a lifetime, her hand slid into a hole in the rock. She grabbed onto the edge and felt she could swim through. It was completely dark in the water, but she swam on until suddenly and quite without warning there was light and she broke through the surface of the water. She swallowed a large breath and cleared the water from her eyes. Looking around she realized she was caught in an air bubble.

"Well, that is a miracle," she said out loud to only herself. She began to look around for the source of the light but found nothing that could create it. She pulled her long form out of the water and on to what could pass for a sandy shoreline. Lexia wanted to rest more than she wanted to fetch this urn, but she knew this needed to be a quick operation and Ares wouldn't wait just because she was a little tired. The air was humid and her wet suit didn't stand a chance of actually drying. She moved around the cave looking for the little entrance where she'd stowed the urn. Surely no one could have found it; the water would have been high enough to block the mouth of the cave for a thousand years if not more.

Lexia began digging in the sand where she thought she had left the urn, noticing the sand had probably risen causing it to be covered as well. Her hand hit pay dirt a foot down. The opening was just large enough for her to lie on her belly and crawl in. She felt the roundness of the urn and hooked her arm around it as she backed out of the small space. With her tongue between her teeth, she completed her task and smiled proudly. She washed the dirt away and pried open the lid wanting to check for her prize before leaving. She wasn't up for round two of hide and go seek. There it lay in the nest of linen she had hidden it with so long ago. A small shaft with cogs attached in different areas along it, and with a small green jewel at both ends. Fitting the lid back in place, she walked into the water and found her exit.

***

On top of the cliff, Lilika and Gelesia stood

shaking their heads as their friend and lover went head first into the water with a giant splash the waves immediately covered. So much for a game plan, Lilika shook her head and sat down dangling her legs over the edge.

"All we can do now is wait. When she reaches the cave it should be all lit up if Uncle Herc got my message through."

"Yeah, well, if she could die I would kill her. Jumping in like that without even a way back up or taking any kind of light. She could be eaten up by the fishes!" Gelly stomped back and forth.

"Oh, come have a seat, dear heart. You know she will be fine." Lilika patted the ground next to her. Gelesia sat down still steaming and rested her head on Lilika's shoulder.

She sighed loudly. "That doesn't help, Lil." Lilika put her arm around the girl and they watched the sun make its way across the sky.

They were laid back on the grass dozing when they heard Lexia's very frustrated yell. Both women bolted upright and on to their feet looking over the edge. Half way up the cliff climbed Lexia. They waved down to her, smiling sheepishly as Lexia rolled her eyes at them.

"Give me a hand would ya? Catch!" She tossed the urn with her right hand straight into the air. Lilika caught it with a surprised look.

"This is it? The piece I have is much bigger."

"It isn't the size that matters. Just ask me," Lexia said climbing over the edge up to their feet with Gelesia bending down to help.

Lexia laid flat on her back resting and letting Lilika make an inspection. The sun dried her wet suit and she found some clothes to put on that weren't as confining.

They mounted their horses and headed away from the cliff.

"I was thinking I could transport us back. It should be safe because we have the piece. Should we ride for a day or have we all had enough of memory lane?"

"I think we've had enough," both women said in unison. Lilika laughed and suddenly the light surrounded them, then they were in front of the gates.

Lilika whistled and the stable boy appeared to fetch the horses, taking them around the house to the pasture. They walked in on foot with Lilika leading the way. "We're back!" she said looking around wondering where everyone could be. Amynta came bounding out of the study doors. "You must go to Olympus immediately!" she shouted. Lilika tossed Lexia the urn and along with it the knowledge of where to put it as she flashed out of this plain.

***

She reappeared before Zeus's throne and realized the whole pantheon was in attendance along with Adriana. Lilika bowed before Zeus. "Grandfather, why are we here?" she said with her eyes lowered but still trying to sneak a look at Adriana who stood by Hercules looking more frightened by the minute. Zeus said nothing but only raised his hands in supplication. A grating and overly cocky voice from behind Lilika pulled her to her feet.

"We are here because I have challenged you. The pieces for your life and the life of this mortal child." He crossed his arms and looked smug.

"Well, I don't know how you expect to kill me but let's go." Lilika drew her sword and took a stance with her wings spread to their full width. She heard Adriana gasp but chose to ignore everything but the arrogant god in front of her. If he did have a way to kill her then everything she had built would be lost along with quite possibly the entire planet. She was determined to save them all and lock Ares away where he could never be found. That would be her forcing Zeus's hand, but so be it. Something must be done to this foolish god. In her mind's eye she saw the great wheel of the Fates turning with their scissors poised to cut a string. Of course they would send an ominous vision now she thought with a wry smile.

Ares ran screaming with his sword over his head bringing the weight of it down with both arms, snarling as Lilika brought her sword up and blocked his frontal assault. She pushed him back and planted her foot firmly in his chest sending him flying across the room hitting the wall with a thud. He was on his feet and both were running full force at the other. They jumped and their swords clashed in the air, ringing over Olympus and sending sparks flying in all directions. Lilika used her wings to force herself down over Ares and push him to his knees as he fought to block the onslaught of blows from her sword. The gods gathered around them and Zeus smiled triumphantly thinking the tides were turning in their favor.

Ares parried and spun on his knees out of her reach. Lilika followed only to be backed up by a fist connecting with her chin. She stumbled then used her wings to propel her forward landing her sword in Ares's gut.

"Really?" he said pulling out a dagger and slicing Lilika's arm. She whirled around pulling her sword through his side, splitting it open and spilling his blood on the floor. He healed almost immediately, laughing as Lilika presented him with blow after blow knocking him again and again down to the marble floor. His face was bloodied and purple when he rose up still laughing. "Getting weak, are we?"

Lilika looked at her arm. It hadn't healed like it should have as Ares face was healing even as she stared at her arm. She looked between Ares and her arm the world around her becoming blurry and spinning. She heard Adriana scream as she blacked out.

Ares loomed over Lilika's prone body as Adriana, in spite of herself, ran to cover her with her own body no matter Ares' intention. His sword was poised in the air for the death strike he had so been longing to blow, not knowing for sure if the poison from the knife was enough to kill her. The combination of poison and the removal of her head should be enough to end her life he thought, releasing a yawp.

"Ares. Enough!" Zeus' voice boomed through the throne room. Ares stopped and looked at his father. His sword flew from his hand and chains wrapped themselves around him appearing as if from nowhere.

"You have forced my hand for the last time. You will spend eternity in your brother's realm, doomed to watch your miserable failures forever." Zeus waved his hand and Ares disappeared along with Hades in a flash of beautiful red light.

"Take her home, Hercules. Time will tell." Hercules flashed them back to Lilika's mansion on the cliffs of Greece.

***

Hercules appeared in the courtyard with Lilika in his arms and Adriana by his side. Immediately, Gelesia was firing questions at the tall god.

"How did this happen? What is wrong with her? Where is Ares?" Hercules made a face requesting silence and asked that they follow him. He carried Lilika to her study and placed her on the couch by the fireplace at the far end of the room. He removed her armor and gave it to Effemia who took it to be cleaned while ignoring her own tears that were running down her face. In the courtyard, all the house staff had gathered and waited anxiously for her to speak. She merely shook her head and took her bundle to the weapons room.

Back inside the study, Hercules sat at Lilika's desk. "Ares is taken care of. Father has doomed him to eternity in Tartarus. He poisoned her, but he only managed to get a little into her system. We will know in a matter of days whether she will come out the other side or be lost to darkness forever."

Gelesia collapsed into Lexia's arms crying silently. The only other person in the world she couldn't bear to lose and never thought she would, may very well die and at the hand of a complete failure. Lexia sat stone faced wondering if there was something she could do. Some medicine, some herb, or modern medical miracle that would do the trick. In the end, she knew it would have to run its course and there was nothing to do but wait.

"But she is a god. How is this happening? I don't understand!" Adriana all but screamed. She had been crying and watching to try and understand but she just couldn't. She looked to Hercules who had been a man of certain answers but he just shook his head. Adriana ran to the couch where Lilika lay. The goddess was sweating and breathing quick shallow breaths. Adriana wiped her face and wept in the floor beside the couch.

No one moved for several hours. Adriana stared at the pale goddess, Hercules sat at the desk occasionally wringing his hands after wiping a tear here or there. Lexia held Gelesia, never taking her eyes off of the patterned rug that was under their feet. A knock at the door roused them from their grieving stupors. It was Effemia and she had a woman with her.

"Excuse me, but I have brought someone who may be of assistance. She is from the village. Amynta requested that I bring her. She stands guard outside the door with Artemis and Aphrodite." They entered the room fully, and Effemia set down a tray laden with food, wine, and tea. Hercules motioned for Adriana to find something on the tray as Lexia and Gelesia followed suit. The woman didn't speak to them but walked over to the sleeping goddess and bent down to inspect her.

"My name is Kallias, Goddess Lilika. I am a doctor for mortals. I hope to make you more comfortable," she said pushing her blonde curls out of her blue eyes. She opened her bag and pulled out a syringe filled with a liquid slightly yellow in color. She looked to the group gathered for any sign of disapproval then plunged the syringe into the goddess's upper arm. She was slightly surprised it pierced the skin and assumed it was the weakened state of her. Emptying the liquid into the goddess, she asked Effemia to get a cold cloth.

"I would much prefer to put her in a cold bath but if she is this weak she could drown," she said to those gathered.

"I can carry her if you are willing to get in with her. I can chill the fountain. It won't take much," Hercules said. Seeing that Kallias was in agreement, he picked up the goddess and carried her to the fountain. Kallias emptied her pockets onto a nearby table and pulled off her shoes and jacket.

"I will need it to be as cold as we can get it without the water freezing. My theory is if we can slow the poison by thickening the blood, it may stop the progression long enough for it to burn the poison out. I gave her a natural clotting agent which may or may not work on gods." She climbed into the water and Hercules put Lilika into the fountain leaned up against Kallias. He waved his hand over the water and chilled it immediately. Kallias drew in a sharp breath. The house staff hung back but stayed within viewing distance while Hercules, Gelesia, and Lexia stood around the fountain. After a few minutes, Kallias asked for her stethoscope and listened to Lilika's heart. It had slowed considerably and she wondered just how long she could handle this water. Her extremities were already numb and on their way to being a color of blue they should never be. She waited another few minutes then listened again. The thudding of the goddess's heart had slowed to a thud every few seconds.

"Let's get her out and put the fire out. Open the windows and lay her on the marble floor of the balcony in the study. Can a breeze be created?" she asked as Lexia was helping her out of the fountain. Artemis took care of the breeze as everyone made their way to the small balcony. There was only room for three people and after the doctor had changed and Aphrodite had warmed her seeing that no harm came to her human appendages, she joined them on the balcony causing Hercules to relinquish his place. No one noticed Adriana had disappeared.

The night passed into morning and the doctor excused herself for some food after checking Lilika's pulse again. No one had slept nor said a word. Eros had shown up and even he was quiet. As the sun rose in earnest, Lexia cleared her throat.

"She hasn't started to sweat again so that has to be a good sign." The good doctor Kallias agreed. She was hoping her plan had worked. It was after all very risky.

The next few days passed much in this respect and without anyone noticing Adriana had gone. The doctor had taken up residence in the study with Effemia making up one of the couches as a makeshift bed. The servants still dropped in but had resumed their daily schedules. Artemis and Gelesia never left Lilika's side. When the doctor would come to check on her, Artemis would stand on the railing of the balcony so she wouldn't be forced to be too far from her beloved daughter.

Lexia and Hercules spent their time conferring and wondering if the sentence Zeus gave Ares was enough. They wanted him to pay with his life and believed he should. Zeus himself never showed his face at Lilika's mansion. Hercules thought him to be too ashamed for not doing something sooner and ignoring Hercules pleas to stop Ares and his foolish, possibly deadly, plan.

***

It had been four days and still there was no change. Early on the fifth day when the doctor checked her heart it had resumed a normal pace. She unwrapped Lilika's arm to check the wound to find it was only a light colored scar that would most likely disappear soon enough.

"How is she?" Gelesia spoke for the group upon seeing the doctor's surprise.

"I believe she is out of the woods. Her wound has healed and her heart is what I can only assume is a normal pace. Let's put her on a couch, shall we?" she said motioning for Hercules. Gelesia swooped in and picked Lilika up, carrying her to the couch with what looked like no effort. Everyone gathered around as the doctor took a seat beside the sleeping goddess. She was confident that her remedy had worked. She was cautiously thrilled. Slowly, Kallias placed her fingers on the chest of the goddess and applied pressure while rubbing in a circular motion. After a few seconds she gasped as a hand grabbed her wrist. It was Lilika's hand and her eyes began to flutter open. She smiled at the doctor and noticed everyone around her. Kallias abruptly stood, not being used to being so close to the awake Lilika. Though she had gotten to know her, it was as a sleeping patient and now she felt she needed appropriate distance for the awake patient.

"Aw, shucks," Lilika whispered weakly. Gelesia was hanging on to Lexia and crying. Everyone had flown the coop but Hercules, Gelesia, and Lexia when they realized she was waking up. It was time to bring the news to Olympus.

She began to sit up fully and looked around the room. The servants had gathered outside the door, Effemia being the only one to enter. She stood at the doors waiting to be called upon. She was crying again but this time it was for joy. The doctor walked back to where Effemia stood letting the friends greet the newly revived goddess. They all began to laugh. It was an easy laughter and a sort of release of breath no one knew they had been holding.

"So, I take it there is no war raging in my honor. Grandfather?" she asked, touching the area Ares had cut open with his poison.

"Yes, he damned Ares to an eternity in chains. I just hope it sticks."

Lilika got to her feet. She noticed she was famished and that she smelled food. She hobbled over to the desk and she made her way through the meat and cheese, of which there wasn't much. "Can I get some soup? Maybe some soup and wine?" She looked to Effemia who shook her head and ran out the door. Lilika leaned on the desk. "So, Kallias, you saved my life. I need to know how to properly thank you." Lilika smiled at the woman who was busy staring at the carpet.

"It was my honor, goddess. Really," she demurred.

"No, it was mine." Lilika walked over to her and wrapped her arms around the woman. "Thank you. Thank you," she whispered into Kallias' ear. The doctor shook her head and wrapped her arms around the goddess in return.

Kallias slipped out as Effemia brought in the wine and hot broth for Lilika.

"Where is Adriana?" For the first time everyone noticed the girl was gone. Not even Amynta had seen her go. The dog put her nose to the air. "I can't smell her any more. That can only mean she has left not only the house but the village," Amynta said, puzzled.

Chapter 8 The End

Lilika was dressed in the fashion of those around her. Stylish Parisians sipping luxuriously colored coffees. She sat down at a table and waited for service. A waitress told her in delicate French that someone would be there in a moment. Lilika nodded and observed the beautiful people around her. She didn't know places like this existed outside of 1960s American cinema, but here she sat waiting for service in a Parisian cafe. An older woman with silver hair and white silk gloves sat at the table across from her. Lilika smiled. The woman's wrinkled features turned into a polite, toothless smile and she tilted her head in a greeting. Suddenly the old woman realized who she was staring in the face and she smiled widely showing white even teeth. She left her table and sat at the chair across from Lilika.

"You survived," she said, removing her white gloves and without missing a beat, "You didn't follow me."

Lilika laughed. "I didn't know I was supposed to follow you," she revealed. "You made your decision and I made mine. I did let you keep your memories. Hercules said you wanted it that way."

"So now you have come back? When I am too old

to love you and keep up with you." She made a quick shaky gesture to the wrinkles on her face. It had been fifty years since she saw Lilika and it looked as though the goddess hadn't aged. She still looked every bit the vital young woman.

Adriana had slipped out when everyone was watching Lilika and the doctor in the fountain all those years ago. She emptied her room, leaving only the everybook behind. She went to the village and to the bookseller to see if he could get her to Athens. From Athens she travelled immediately to Paris. She had lived here ever since she left Greece, letting her family believe she had just disappeared. Her father died while still waiting for his little girl to come home. She knew it was wrong but she had changed too much. Those times in Greece with immortals and gods had only worked to drive her over an edge she didn't know she stood at.

She wandered the streets of Paris half insane until she met a man who changed her life. He took her in and saw through her madness. Eventually she stopped talking about all that she had witnessed and began to study theology and had even changed a major fact or two. All of this was under an assumed name and then a married name. She had shaped an entire life in Paris. Never having any children and never longing for any, she and her husband lived quietly until he died a few years ago. Now she sat at this cafe every day. At the table he had noticed her from when she wandered the streets whispering to herself about gods.

"You were happy. I am happy that you were happy."

"What of you?" she asked, surprising Lilika with ancient Greek. She had forgotten nothing in all this time.

"I am happy. I found a new path. I couldn't stay angry at you. It wouldn't have been fair."

This surprised Adriana. This may have been fifty odd years ago for her but she still expected some wrath, even if just a little.

"I'm glad you never came for me even though I looked for your face in every crowd," Adriana said sipping her coffee.

"I knew that wasn't what you wanted. You would have stayed otherwise, yes? I would never want to have you by force."

The goddess and the mortal talked into the evening and then into the night. She explained what happened to Ares had so far stuck. Lilika told her she'd managed to get all of the pieces to the machine he had wanted to build. That if he had succeeded, then he could have brought back all the dead dictators he wanted so he could force his own will over the planet. They laughingly agreed a bullet had been dodged. At midnight, Adriana thought it best to head home. She was an old woman now and didn't have the stamina she once possessed. The goddess walked her to her door, hugging her one last time before disappearing into the night with her arms around a young, oddly familiar looking blonde the old woman had noticed waiting on the sidewalk. Lilika turned to wave once more before heading off down the street.

Later, as the old woman lay in bed, she suddenly knew the face of the blonde. It was the doctor that had done so much to save Lilika but she hadn't aged a day! So that was her new path Adriana thought. The next morning, the maid found Adriana with a smile upon her wrinkled features. Not even death had wiped it away. Lilika and Kallias stood in the shadows, invisible to the eyes around them, watching as the undertaker took her frail body out. They had watched her pass to the other side in her sleep. It was peaceful which made Lilika happy. The maid shuttered the house and locked the door. Adriana's lawyers were taking care of her meager estate. Adriana had left instructions that it all go to her niece, her brother's only child, in the states.

Lilika looked around one last time, breathing in a scent she would never breathe again. Then, she took Kallias by the hand and they left the way they had come in, no one knowing they were ever there, returning to the grand house on the cliff.

Section II

The Journey of Poetry

Contemporary

They are teaching their children to kill
While we sit fat bellied and in justified
condemnation. Teaching
our children how to kill

All isn't artifice with flesh and bone
We forget the consequences of our
arguments. Forget
the bloodied ripped flesh

The comparison of swollen bellied babes
To our swollen heads and peon brains
thickened wallet of waste. Comparison
 of what we know is worse

Bombardment of propaganda
To my phone, my email, the machine
that lights up my post history world.
Bombardment of opinion masquerading
as fact.

I am contemporary.

9/3/2013-10:36pm

My papaw is dying

He was demented before

He was demented

We have spent time

Though not nearly enough

Blaming him

Cajoling him

Medicating him

Bold words from times past

Are now forgotten

In lieu of death

He had become the old man

Who didn't know toilet

Clothes

Food

Or anyone

Now Death

Has come to call

He knew, you know.

Long before us

He knew

And made peace

If not with us

But with his Maker

Conflicted

I miss receiving those back door blowjobs

While the current love of my life waits,

Watching television in the family room

Now I am sterile and responsible

Usually in love and "doing my best"

The shelter of mother's little helper all that

To stop me from being bothered by the sight

And sound of the walls ever so slowly closing in

It's outside my scope of practice but

Why should I mind?

Even when the rewards don't match the sacrifice

I miss my vice

Shit like that only happens when my back

And nose are touching the walls

I'm far too tired to be the bigger person

So I sit in mental squalor, conflicted.

Death

1. Scream
It was piercing
That moment in time
When words separated from emotion
Darkness gorging me
Screaming the only words I knew
Faded muffles and tears of pain
So slow, so small, it was over.
2. Rain
The rain in my head became acidic
As I broke every promise I had made
Blinded, broken by fury
No tomorrow, "I will not have a new day."
It whispers on repeat
So like me to have nothing to live for
Even some demons are just people
3. Revenge
Needing cruelty for revenge
Saving a dead life the ways it's ending
So callous and rough
I have it now, it's not over
You should see me now
Pleasant pretty playmate
My youth has escaped.

Faking Mommy

It's Friday.
Fridays are longer than most days
I wait on Fridays.
I do what is expected…
What we agreed I would do.
Still, my day is all about you.
There is no landslide
No one to hearken
I have me until 1:15
I find I am mostly useless
A bore, a reminiscent old badger
But of what I don't know
The girl at 3 am
The flake, the whores, the steam engine
The one with legs for a mile
When words flowed like wine
And I could drink until the bottle
Was reduced to clear empty glass

Flip Top Box

flip top box
my heart inside a container
great joy, full of feeling
I know nothing
forgot your name
but got your number
tattooed on my tongue
goes right through
the three feet from head to ass
my jealousy contains unfounded beliefs
of a delusional reality
give me water
quench my thirst of you
dance! shake that ass!
you always knew how to move
up and down my little heart
so well dressed
couldn't forget the blues
highlights of life
small pieces of time
getting freaky in the other room
with my flip top box

I Think Not a Soul Mate

I want to hear the broken glass
of last night laid out before me.
Put the pieces in order, so
I can recall it, relay it to you.
Fiend of me. Friend of mine.
Who has my soul if not me?
I gave it away I know not to whom.
For if it was God why does it now burn?
Along with emotion and feeling
out of control inside my head.
 Can I have it back, my soul?
Better care I can take than you.
Devil, his spacious way of making
love on rosy beds of face.
Smelling it burn crackle sizzle
Take me down there if it's here.
I ran from it once shall one day again.
At least I possess it enough
 to never get better.
Honey, pass me the flowers.
Greet me with open arms.
I'll be the hero you be the victim.
I'll be your mother without shame
Come inside black and blue
Give my soul to you?
I just got it from God

The Devil wanted it too
Neither did woo, though, like you.

Lesson

Did you find Heaven
wasn't where it's at?
And that Hell
isn't all it's cracked up to be?
Tell me did you
find your great mistake
Downtown with the Saints?
Kissing Spring marrying June?
Coming up for air
in life's lake of despair.
Among the crowd
wings waving
at little girls in cowboy hats
on the arms of men in drag.
Did you tell God
the Devil wasn't sorry?

New Deity

Civilized steeples
Above angry church people
It's alright to have blue doors
As long as you are a satin worshiper
Make sure in praise odds even out
Cause God won't hear a tainted heart
Serving what they know
Preaching what they feel
Disco balls in new sanctuaries
must match the motif
All in the name of the moment
Do what you do
Top it off with a bit of shame
Can't be lonely, we got the new deity
Sowing wild oats with some prayer
Dancing to that little hymn
Civilized steeples
Built with care of structure
to be insulted with pride
So it's not a game without shame
Much less we must all know the blame

The Devil in Me

I am the one no one should meet.
Been around and around for years
waiting for the moment to take.
Dark alleys sinister and belligerent men
all have nothing on me.
Starting out beautiful, as we all do,
finding my own way to forget predestination.
I remember Nero, bright one he was
Never learned that music and fire don't mix.
Then those consumed with hate
can't forget those for Christ's sake.
Seems too funny, Hitler, that sheep
Going Greek for blonde hair and blue eyes.
I forget now just how it came to be
I think now, though, it was me.
A grand plan, contrary as a mortal
fixated with a green mile.
Maybe I'm wrong but love,
was never more real to me than hate
was known to the Divine Divinity.
All is tasted by everyone, I know.
Let's not forget the gays.
Faithful seekers of love they are.
I swear seems more like Aphrodite's job.
I love, I do, the sun, the moon.
Been there twice, it was nice.

Now, though, this day this hour
I'll lie here and laugh.
Because the temptation is so strong.

The Seeking of One Thing Shall Find Another

Blazing love,
I lost my heart today.
Thought I had thrown it away
Or frozen it on a shelf
Turns out it was hiding itself.
Behind a lung
Is where it hung.
Waiting for the moment
To reinvent and repent
I tossed it far
So the bigger the scar.
While I prayed to sin
Turns out I fell in love again.

White Horse

I saw a white horse on a green hill
The rain drizzled fog swayed in cool air
The horse's eyes stared into my own
I struggled to understand
Eternity in a moment
The drizzle continued and my fear
seemed to fall with it
Soaking deep into my bones
as it soaked my wool coat
The horse stared on
I had to continue

The Whiff of Brimstone

The whiff of brimstone
and wet hands
Electricity of moments
Brain currents and memory
Do I cease to be when I finally
cease to be?
Is it relived with the emotional
detachment of the dead?
A bursting of fury light and sound
leaves my lips
I crash every night
A flash of memory that friend
The one who kept me
Finally slipped away.
Long winded and damned
Surprising words we have
for each other.
For whom, I'm not sure.
Externalizing, a gift,
from a god who hates me.
A whiff of brimstone
and I'm falling again
bottomless pit and surroundings.
Wicked games and screams
A heartless leap for one
so young in heart and old in soul

I can't remember now
if I chose this.
As the ghosts haunt me
ethereal bodies unfocused,
unable to focus mine.
Did I or did someone…
I can't remember.
Or maybe that question
is the wrong question.
The whiff of brimstone
and life left me
unprepared in task, word
and so called deed.
My goal weakened me
I was your pedestal
No one lifted me
led me here.
My time is your toy
A leisurely game of needing
to be needed.
The whiff of brimstone
I still need to hit bottom.

Section III
The Journey of the Stream

Moving Through the Stream

I was walking back down the hall contemplating whether or not it was appropriate to lick the icing off my cinnamon bun. This was my little routine, this contemplation and this walk. I laugh and think the same thing every morning. *Should I? Shouldn't I?* Patient's families are around and can identify me by the surgery cap on my head and the blue scrubs that cover me top and bottom. Even though it is 8 am and my cinnamon bun I must maintain the look of a hospital professional. They watch me walk, follow me with their eyes, afraid that I have news or afraid that I don't.

That isn't my job. Even if the eight hours I spend here consume my life and dictate almost every move I make. These people's sorrow cannot be my own. I have enough life to live without theirs. After I pass through the doors the contemplation is gone and I am me eating my cinnamon bun and drinking my double shot of espresso with crème for the next fifteen minutes. Well, the next twelve, my last three minutes are spent being anxious about losing time.

The day moves forward after that. Fast or slow, at the end of those eight hours I have still earned my money. When I am here, in this hospital, inside these sterile rooms with caps and masks, I feel as if I don't exist. I am an ant doing what I must for the colony. I realize it is my selfishness that keeps me working. The world at large dictating what I perceive to be life. Overhead the loud speaker booms, "We need a bed and PCT to room 12, please."

I clear my mind by locking away my thoughts and report to the room to fulfill my responsibilities. I push the bed to the side of the operating table and help pull the patient over, then the crowd clears and the cleaning begins. Wiping up all the blood and sweeping up the bone. We cover the operating table with a clean sheet and mop our way out of the room as scrub techs are entering to prepare for the next case. We laugh and joke if no other room needs our special brand of attention, then go our separate ways to carry out some other duty until we must all reconvene in another room.

When the work is done I can pretend to be myself again, quietly. I look for something that keeps me alone so I can resume my thoughts. The words and pictures in my mind almost batter me physically. I could be sick on my own thoughts. That makes me smile, to be sick on my own thoughts. It leads me to another time and place where romance was most assuredly born. A time where poetry rolled off the tongues of lovers and friends like spit. I am suddenly lost, floating through fog like a ghost completely unaware of my current predicament.

Just when the muse is set to smile upon me, the loud speaker booms overhead. Life starts up again outside of my fog. I am once again corporeal. Three different voices call out one after the other, "We need a PCT to the front desk, please." The please sounded like an afterthought to make us feel as though we aren't the help here to be at their beck and call. The next voice needs a bed to room seven and calls out as I am passing by on my way to the desk. I choose to clean the room instead, and by choose I mean I am closer to room seven than I am the desk and I should have a choice in the matter, shouldn't I? I try to let the thought that I have a choice placate me as I gather what I need for the room. The warm blankets for the patient, the clean sheets, and the rag for the bed. I sigh and enter the room. I decide to wait on the trash bags, linen bags, and suction canisters figuring that will take more time from my day. I move the stretcher into the room slowly, cautiously, this is a small room and I don't want to jar the operating table. Then the nurse grabs the foot of the stretcher and helps guide it into place. I'm grateful and politely say thank you. She is new and I am unfamiliar with her.

Eventually more PCTs filter in and we move the patient with confident and practiced hands. After the patient is wheeled out, we go about our cleaning. The satellite radio in the room is on a station that plays music from the 1980s and we begin to sing along to Prince's *Purple Rain*. One of the guys helping me clean is a total prick most of the time but right now he is just the guy leading the sing along, pretending the mop handle is a microphone. As the song ends we all end up laughing. One of the PCTs says we need to get the room done and tries not to sound like he loves bossing people around. When he turns to walk out of the room, we salute him with our middle fingers.

The prick turns to me and says, "Even if that guy *is* the lead PCT, he would be pissed if he knew what a joke everyone thinks he is." I laugh and admit he probably already knows since he has eyes and ears everywhere, my words dripping with sarcasm. We finish the room and I walk idly back to another room to see if they need help finishing up. Lucky for me they are finished and hauling out the trash and linen.

Starting off down the hallway to find something to occupy my time when my friend Sophie comes up beside me. We fall into a common step and begin to chat quickly in case her pint-sized boss happens by.

"So I am going to have a thing here soon. Play some cards and drink a little. It should be fun."

I agree to come as long as she doesn't get me as drunk as she did the last time and I end up vomiting everywhere. By everywhere, I mean the side of the road on the drive home, my best friend's driveway, his hand, and his mother's den. I grin. "To be a straight lady, you sure are good at getting girls drunk."

She laughs. "Just you, my little lesbian fart." We giggle like the girls we are until we spy her boss heading our way. We fall out of step and the moment of laughter and friendship is lost.

I head to my locker to grab my knife. We are nearly out of foam and the act of cutting it is a solitary one. I walk into the locker room and realize it is empty. I can't resist the red padded chair that is next to the door. I sit down enjoying the release of tension in my lower back and legs. The silence of the room floods my ears and I am happy. I glance to the clock on the wall and then to my watch. I snort; I will always be a clock watcher. It was nearly 10:45 which meant it was nearly my lunch time. Water and a cigarette, the lunch of champions, I snort again. Keeping my butt in the seat a little longer, I convince myself nothing is going on so I can stay seated for a few more minutes. Just then the door opens and Sandra, a tall very slight nurse comes strolling in. "Hey, kid," she says to me. I smile and return her greeting.

She passed through the door opposite of where I sit. My mind began to wander— Sandra is more than 20 years older than me but she radiates cool in a way that most people never do. She could be Danny from *Grease* or The Fonz from *Happy Days*. But she just has what those boys never could to go along with her coolness, and that is the mystery of a woman. Maybe it was her silence and that ability to speak in such a way that it caused people to listen when she decided to do so. She was someone my young mind said I should emulate and compare myself to. I checked the clock again, 15 minutes until 11 am. I go seek out the *lead PCT* and inform him that I am heading to lunch, my intentions to cut foam completely forgotten.

He was standing with his hands on his hips, speaking emphatically to another PCT who was looking amused but holding the boredom in his eyes we all have when the *lead* speaks to us. There were only eight of us which often makes the work day difficult, but we love and hate each other all the same. I tell him my lunch time intention, trying to hide the ridiculousness of having to inform him. He shakes his head and continues his rant to the other man standing with him, the two men having been in a pissing contest probably since they began working together some twenty odd years before. Much like all the others in this operating room, they have a love hate relationship. The only difference being, the *lead PCT* is disliked by everyone and the other guy isn't. He makes an effort to make everyone smile and always has a joke or two to tell.

As I hit the exit door it is forgotten, and by the time I am waiting on the elevator in the parking garage, I am smiling. I make my way to my car and realize for the first time today the heat. It was well over 90 degrees and I was sweating. I rolled down my windows and turned the radio low after lighting my first cigarette since 6 that morning. I exhaled happily then heard the hospital's trauma helicopter and my happiness is dampened. The noise drowned out the radio then, but created a nice breeze. I had an idle fear of it crashing on my car or worse, somewhere close to where I parked and I wouldn't be killed just badly burned. I shrugged; it would get me out of work. It was a dreadful thought that only the fatigued and desensitized could justify. I hated being so blasé about my own wellbeing just so my time wouldn't be eaten away by others. Keeping up with the injured train of thought, I would have time to write and time to think. It could make me brilliant or it could make me nothing. Either way, it would be something tangible that I could wear on my sleeve so I could put my heart back into my chest.

Throwing the cigarette butt out the window, I started fiddling with the radio trying to find some song to soothe my mind. I lit another cigarette and took a large gulp of water then looked to the clock. Only fifteen minutes of peace left. The helicopter flew back overhead; after it faded geese soon followed honking to each other. I wondered if geese argued like people argue. Is that what they were honking about? Was I hearing a geese pissing contest? Maybe they were arguing over where to go or where had the better food. I threw out the second cigarette butt and looked at the clock again. Five minutes left to myself. The day was bright and hot with only a few puffy white clouds. I hoped for rain on days this hot. Living in a house without air conditioning could become stifling on days like this. The concrete and bricks that made up my house only had heat to soak up and I had a treeless yard. I exited the car figuring I better make it back so I didn't get spanked for taking a few extra minutes on lunch.

Upon arriving back into the hallowed halls of the operating room, all I could hear was the loud speaker booming with need. The need for patients to be fetched, beds to be brought, and rooms to be cleaned. My pager, or leash as most of us called them, was vibrating on my hip. Room 14 needed me and I knew no one else would go. I shrugged; so much for brushing my teeth.

Even though it ate into my time to think, I liked being this busy. It made time move swiftly and we all seemed to work as a unit. A task to keep us being obedient ants. It was a beautiful dance, this common goal of moving people and brooms and bones. The room to which I headed was never bloody or littered with bone chips or gobs of congealed blood clots. Mostly it was used to

147

remove bladder or kidney stones. The beds were huge with a large x-ray machine attached to them with a clear plastic bag with a drain tube at the end. So even though it wasn't a bloody room, it reeked of urine. The smell of urine was something you didn't notice after a while, just like blood and burnt flesh became common smells. I finished the room by replacing the bag at the end of the bed and mopping my way out. I hung the mop up outside of the room in the neat little rack designed for this purpose and headed back through the doors to the main operating room.

At the front of the hall ahead of me a small crowd had gathered. A patient had crashed and ultimately died. Those of us who were of no use in the remainder of the situation drifted away to other areas or tasks. I headed to the other side of our square hall to a room that needed attention. The friendliest PCT that everyone loved was there ready to be of assistance and making the nurses giggle. I was thoughtful as we cleaned the room. Those around me were saying the organs may be harvested as late as tomorrow and we all groaned because that made for quite a mess. Even though we felt for the family, we could keep our detachment by focusing on our work and our work was the cleanup. The whole world could be affected by the death in that room but we are the ones who have to clean it up. Death of a patient was the only thing that remained for us that day. It didn't happen very often, and when it did, we all became louder or more perverse or meaner that day.

I thought of a teacher I had in high school. His motto was *no one gets out of here alive so make the best of it*. We finished the room and went to wait at the dead man's room. They were going to harvest his organs today. The donation team had already been called and soon strangers would be invading our private island and taking with them something more precious than gold. It was a waiting game. By two pm the harvest team had arrived and we were geared up to put our hands on death. After they finished with the body it was us who had to clean it and put it in a white body bag disguised with a sheet so the family could see him off to his destination. I was glad to not see the family. We milled around pretending to not think of our own mortality while waiting for the team to finish. My thoughts at lunch came back to me along with the guilt of those thoughts. Death wasn't ordinary; whatever travesty happened to this man may have been, but his death was not.

By 4 o'clock they hadn't finished and it was time for us to leave. We breathed a sigh of relief. It wouldn't be us we must have thought collectively as we went to the locker rooms to change into our street clothes. I threw on jeans and a t-shirt along with a baseball cap. OR caps don't do your hair any favors. We gathered at the time clock, our badges in hand, waiting for the minute to strike when we could slide our plastic cards and receive our evening's freedom. I slid my card and welcomed the silence that would soon fill my ears. My day was over and my time was mine to do with as I please.

www.ingramcontent.com/pod-product-compliance
Lightning Source LLC
Chambersburg PA
CBHW052009240626
47153CB00008B/2804